STARFIELD

SCIENCE FICTION by SCOTTISH WRITERS

STARFIELD

THE ANTHOLOGY OF SCIENCE FICTION BY SCOTTISH WRITERS

EDITED BY DUNCAN LUNAN

ORKNEY PRESS
KIRKWALL 1989

Published by The Orkney Press Ltd 1989. 12 Craigiefield Park, St Ola, Kirkwall, Orkney

Designed and typeset by Dog & Bone, Glasgow
Cover by Sydney Jordan, illustrating *The Rig* by Chris Boyce
Printed by The Orcadian, Victoria Street, Kirkwall, Orkney

The following works first appeared in these publications listed with them — *The Rig* by Chris Boyce in SF Impulse no.7, September 1966: *A Continuing Experiment* by Janice Galloway in *The Glasgow Herald,* June 20, 1987: *Busman's Holiday* by Louise Turner in *The Glasgow Herald,* July 30, 1988: *What Dreams May Come* by Angus McAllister in *Woman* magazine, October 28, 1978: *The Particle Poems* and *The Moons of Jupiter* by Edwin Morgan in *Star Gate*: science fiction poems by Edwin Morgan, Third Eye Centre, Glasgow, 1979, and in *Poems of Thirty Years,* Carcanet Press, 1982: *The Dowser* by Edwin Morgan in *Two Tongues – Two Towns*, ed. Reinard Knodt and Jack Withers, Dagyeli Verdag, 1988, and in *Themes on a Variation,* Carcanet Press, 1988: Prof. Morgan's poems appear by permission of Carcanet Press Ltd: *Spaced Out* by David Crooks in The Glasgow Herald, March 29, 1986: *Venjinss* by Alburt Plethora in Culture City, Issue 38, March 1989: *The Crank that Made the Revolution* by Alasdair Gray in The Scottish Field, 1971, and *The Cause of Some Recent Changes* in Ygorra, 1957. Both are included in *Unlikely Stories, Mostly,* Canongate,1983: *The Square Fella* by Duncan Lunan in *The Glasgow Herald,* April 1, 1989.

ISBN 0 907618 21 9
The publishers acknowledge subsidy from the Scottish Arts Council towards the publication of this volume.

OTHER BOOKS by DUNCAN LUNAN

DEDICATED TO
STEVEN PROSTERMAN
WHO WANTED TO ENCOURAGE
SCOTTISH WRITERS

TABLE OF

CONTENTS

INTRODUCTION
Angus MacVicar

SCIENCE FICTION DEALS EITHER WITH WHAT MIGHT have been or what might be. It measures in an imaginative and exciting way the ability of *homo sapiens* to come to terms with his physical environment and to control his destiny. In this respect it does not differ widely from orthodox fiction. The special ingredient it contains – an ingredient which most orthodox fiction lacks – is a catholic knowledge of science.

It contains also another ingredient which could be said to be sadly lacking in some orthodox fiction, especially that of the modern, 'shock 'em with sex and violence' variety: the ingredient of good storytelling. This is brilliantly exemplified in the works of literary giants of the past like Robert Louis Stevenson with *Dr Jekyll and Mr Hyde,* H.G.Wells with *The Time Machine* and Sir Arthur Conan Doyle with *The Lost World.*

It is an art form as old as history: indeed, as old as prehistory.

Some of the earliest science fiction is to be found in the Bible. In the first chapter of his book the prophet Ezekiel described the approach to earth of a space vehicle containing strange creatures: 'four with the face of a man, another with the face of a lion, four with the face of an ox, and four also with the face of an eagle.' He is so taken up with this astonishing story that he repeats it in Chapter 10.

(Is it possible that Ezekiel's 'vision' was based on fact? From the details he provides a present-day scientist has made a working model of the vehicle concerned.)

The Book of Revelation is science fiction from beginning to end. St John's account of the cosmic battle waged between the forces of good and evil (Christ and the Devil) is a magnificent example of the art. His purpose was to suggest that in the end the struggle between the 'angels' and the 'beasts' will result in angelic victory. He was also determined to assure his readers that we live not in a mad chaos, as it sometimes seems, but in a planned universe built upon a scientifically enhanced spiritual foundation in which love predominates. The best of science fiction follows this line of approach. It is not afraid to offer 'messages,' some overt, some subliminal, as encouragement – and perhaps also warning – to the human race. This anthology demonstrates how boldly Scottish writers have entered the lists. Most of them avoid a common failing in what may be called 'pulp' science fiction, an almost complete absence of character drawing. A collection of cardboard characters lost in a maze of scientific data does not constitute science fiction. Ezekiel and St John made sure that science remains in the service of humanity.

Compiling this book has been a labour of love for Duncan Lunan over the past five years. He himself is a distinguished practitioner in the field, and the quality of his scientific publications gives him an authority to judge other writers and make a choice. I am sure this project will have the success his enthusiasm deserves.

I take some pride in Duncan Lunan's kind admission that my science fiction radio and television serials broadcast in the BBC's Children's Hour in the 1950s – and the *Lost Planet* books which later became best-sellers all over the world – helped to fire his childhood ambition to become a science writer.

Those *Lost Planet* serials were all produced in the Glasgow studios of the BBC by that wonderful lady, Kathleen Garscadden. Because children always deserve the best and, in any case, can spot phonies more readily than adults, I was careful to make the scientific background as accurate as possible. I was also glad to follow Kathleen's strong suggestion that there should be what she called 'an ethic' in all the stories. The little white flowers of 'charity' found on Hesikos, the lost planet, were the product of that suggestion.

I remember the excitement in the studio during the live broadcast of the first *Lost Planet* episode. No science fiction serial had been attempted before in Children's Hour and much depended upon the success of newly minted sound effects, especially the sound effects constructed for the launching of the space ship.

This was composed of recordings of the Victoria Falls interspersed with the roar of John Cobb's record-breaking speedboat on Loch Ness. Kathleen was afraid it might lack conviction. She need not have worried. Children wrote in to say what a thrilling sound it was and demanding more *Lost Planet* stories, year by year.

Duncan Lunan was among them. And now, in an age much more sophisticated in regard to science and sound effects, it is his turn to launch a science fiction venture in the shape of this book. I applaud it and wish it well.

Angus MacVicar.

There is, I believe, a distinctive quality to speculative fiction produced by Scottish writers. It's a blend of the mystical Celtic background with the national tradition of science and engineering. It generates science fiction with a strong sense of atmosphere, and fantasy with convincing detail. It's no coincidence that so many of us write in other fields, many of us in non-fiction. After his novels Catchworld *(winner of the Gollancz/Sunday Times prize) and* Brainfix *Chris Boyce published the non-fiction* Extraterrestrial Encounter, *and his shorter work has as many non-fiction credits as fiction.*

Chris appeared on the SF scene with three major pieces in the magazine SF Impulse, 1966-97. *Despite the impression they made at the time none of them has been reprinted, so we begin here with* The Rig, *which on its first appearance was ilustrated by Keith Roberts. Our cover is by Sydney Jordan, himself a Scot, and creator of the world's longest-running SF cartoon strip,* Jeff Hawke.

Chris Boyce
THE RIG

'YOU LOOK DISGUSTING.'

Plus raw ill and nauseated into the bargain.

'Yes. I was sick in the helicopter, Sir Martin.'

From behind his desk he looks up at you with his black button eyes. He is a little man, but taller than you, bald with tufts of wiry white hair above the red protruding ears, and sitting in an overstuffed armchair, his small chubby hands folded across his pot belly, he worries the cuff of his right sleeve with his left thumb.

'Couldn't you have changed or cleaned yourself up? Good God, man, you're smelling!'

'I know sir. Soya beans with ... garlic powder.'

— Delicious too.

'Ugh. Clear out of my office and don't come near me or the lab shack until you're decent. Understand?'

Nod.

'Yes Sir Martin.'

'Clear off I said, Mr. Jalovec. Clear off!'

Walk nippily out of the door.

Out to where the mad sea winds howl round the rig in wild glee, and Scotland lies ninety miles westward. Look over the rail, down to where the heady grey waves burst themselves to bubbles and cream against the scum covered expanse of the sea lily.

The sea lily extending wide and darkly about this island of steel on stilts. Afloat down there, all three of its broad enormous leaves spreading out from where they are anchored to the legs of the rig. Hundreds of feet across lying out on the North Sea.

What is it? An offbeat green fungus with a twisted sense of humour maybe?

Unlikely.

But that is what you are here to find out.

The popular press christened it 'Sea Lily' even although it bears not the slightest resemblance to the actual marine plant of that name.

And of course everyone has his own pet theory about it.

A plant spore blown high above the Martian atmosphere by a volcanic eruption is caught up in the current of Mariner IV's radio signals to earth and is carried across space to drop into the North Sea almost a year later.

Radioactive waste from a nuclear submarine mutates a common seaweeed into a flat glaucous leviathan.

This oil rig *Sea Horse* while drilling loosed from some deep sub-strata a buried seed belonging to a species of marine life which became extinct over one thousand million years ago.

It's this younger generation, the Devil, and the hydrogen bomb.

Maybe it is this younger generation.

A hoax.

That is the only explanation that might make sense.

Now what college or university has a 'rag day' about now. Coming to think on it some of those samples which you had flown in from here definitely looked as if they had been tampered with.

Your shoulder is being shaken. The second radio operator with

straggly long brown hair dangling over his pale quartzose face.
'What are you hanging over the edge for? Are you going to be
sick again?' trying to get upwind from you.

At the mention a small hairy goblin skips up your large intestine
and starts to thump the wall of your stomach with sadistic gusto.
'Well if you're not going to spew come on with me. I'm starving
with the cold out here and I'm dying to climb into my kip.'

Once inside you move along straight narrow passages, the
constant grumble of the drilling sounding louder here with no
winds to disperse it. The noise seems to quiver from the chairs in
the saloon as you pass, from the beds in the dormitory, from the
floorboards ceiling and walls.

'This is your place.'

The cabin door is pushed aside to reveal what looks like a
converted cupboard with table, chair, and makeshift bunk-bed.

'Wash those clothes pretty soon mister, or they'll stink you to
death in this wee hole.'

He leaves.

Good advice. Off with the macintosh and start peeling those
sticky drawers away from your pallid greasy thighs. The stench
curls up into your nostrils again. Your guts palpitate excitedly.

— Hold your breath, lad.

As the pressure swells you stumble frantically for the sink, grab
it by the sides, and imagine the bilious face of Sir Martin Amherst
gawking up at you from the plughole.

Smile.

— Standby for torpedoes ...
... FIRE ONE ...
... FIRE TWO ...
(messy misfire that time.)
... FIRE THREE ...
' ... aaah.'

— Cherish the thought.

After a half hour of washing, scrubbing with a nailbrush, and
general redressing you start out for the lab shack to meet the other
two research scientists working with the lily mystery. Rounding

a corner you are confronted with a grinning faceful of semi-decayed teeth.

'Ah. You'll be Jalovec, old Goodwin's replacement.'

'Yes.'

'Oh good. I'm Ernest Prescott. We'll be working together with Dr Daily.'

Shake his offered hand with your friend-confidant type grip.

'I may be wrong but weren't you a couple of forms below me at Scarsdale, Jalovec?'

'You must be mistaken. I went to Uddingston Grammar, outside Glasgow.'

'Oh. I'm sorry.'

A small silence.

'I, er, I read your paper on the spawning season of the *Idiacanthus Fasciola,* fascinating Dr Prescott.'

'It was rather good wasn't it? Three years of work went into that you know.'

'Really?'

'Yes, but it was worth it in the end of course. Now if you'll follow me I'll take you out to the lab shack. This way Mr Jalovec.'

Up a steel ladder, through a hatch, and onto the top of the rig. The sound of the drilling diminishes slightly and rises a little in pitch from a muffled groaning to a grating mechanical overture. Over there the derrick is glistening where the hard white evening lights shine on its towering drizzle-wet struts. The web of a titan black spider run mad.

'What progress have you made so far?' Shouting at him through the wailing wind.

'Practically none I'm afraid … can you hear me?'

'Just.'

'The work is terribly frustrating, you know. I think that's what finally became too much for old Goodwin. Nervous breakdown. He's in a funny-factory now.'

'How did it happen?'

'Well he started acting jittery, talking to himself and so on, decidedly odd. Then one evening — Here we are, you go through

first.'
  'Thank you.'
      — Yumm. Lovely inside. Cumfy and warm
  'Hang your raincoat up on the arm of that switch. We never use it. Anyway, about Goodwin.
  'One night about three weeks ago he climbed down onto the lily with a gallon drum of ethyl alcohol and an axe. Started chopping away at the flesh and pouring alcohol into the wounds. Screaming and sobbing all the time. Sounded like someone being tortured to us. That is why we ran out to see what was going on, and looked down just as he set light to it all.
  'Luckily we managed to extinguish the flames before any serious damage was done. Poor fellow. He kept babbling on about the lily being out to enslave him, enslave us all. He was put under heavy sedation and flown away next day.'
      — Always knew Goodwin was turned
        He would beat his wife because
        He could 'hear' her being
        Unfaithful to him in her
        Dreams.
        Psychic,
        Or psychotic.
  'Dr Daily?'
  'I'm over here Ernest, at the Stereoscan.'
      — Woman's voice.
  She steps out from behind the enamelled bulk of the electron microscope. Gaze vacuously into these long-lashed green eyes, and the red hair falling in a volcanic cascade across her brow and shoulders.
      — Perfect everything.
        Nice, very nice.
  She reaches out and clasps your hand. Her fingers seem to fasten themselves into your skin like steel spring-clips, leaving white marks slowly turning red. Amazed you stare at your hand flexing it slowly, painfully, while the lady regards you with a look of cool satisfaction.

— God. She's strong.

'Has Ernest been acquainting you with our lack of progress —'

'I've told him how frustrating it is Fenella.'

'Have you told him how you still aren't sure yet whether it's flora or fauna, but then you are rather stupid in a charming sort of way. I personally don't think that it's either frankly.'

'*Uh?*'

'Don't stand there with your mouth open like a mute midget, Jalovec my love. Look intelligent. Do something. Here, read these.'

She pushes a pile of pale yellow papers into your arms.

'Our reports for the past two months.'

'But I've read them, Dr Daily.'

'That's what you think, little friend. Take a look at, er … Here this will do for an example. What is it?'

Long look.

Upside down?

More long looks.

Thinks:

Stinks.

'It looks like a photograph of a chloroplast.'

'Clever boy, but have you ever seen chloroplasts two inches across?'

'But that's impossible. They're microscopic …'

'A lot of things are impossible, like an organism with no nucleic acids, no enzymes, no proteins. Correct Ernest?'

'Oh yes quite correct. Even the chlorophyll in those giant chloroplasts is new to us. It isn't type a or type b, and it has far too much magnesium in it for my liking.'

'We send samples away with every helicopter but they only lead to confusion.'

'I don't understand Dr Daily. All the samples that were flown in to us contained traces of all these things which you say are missing. Furthermore we didn't receive any samples containing chlorophyll or these chloroplasts.'

'Naturally. Sweet Sir Martin has strong views about what is biologically 'right' and 'wrong', so he spends all his time up in his little office 'doctoring' all the land bound samples. Mental corrosion. He's only fit for politics. Am I right, Ernest?'

'Of course, Fenella. The only reason he's here is because he got in everyone's hair at the Maxwell Research Unit.'

'When we came out at first he was madly enthusiastic, but now with his imagination exhausted, his potential is completely depleted. His liquor cabinet however has become the centre of activity, for him by day and for another party by night. A party who always manages to sneak in about twice a week and become blind drunk. Don't you Ernest darling?'

'Why, eh? ... well, er ... '

'You see Jalovec the crew despise poor Ernest and Sir Martin is not pleased with his work, and to crown it all I have not fallen victim to his irresistible charms. It's all just too much for your delicate ego isn't it my sweet?'

'Really, ha, ha, Fenella you will have your little jokes. The trouble with Sir Martin is simply that the Minister is making things uncomfortable for him. It makes him irritable.'

'And what about the crew? I suppose that the geologists are jealous of your doctorate, and the rest simply envy your intelligence and education.'

'Well, yes. It's obvious. Isn't it?'

'To you it is.'

'To anyone, Fenella. Why most of them are just superstitious seamen. Why they even think that the pull of the ocean currents on the sea lily will bring the rig down, Jalovec.'

— GULP
          Thinking of *Sea Gem*.
          Something like a dozen people
          Dead.

'B-b-but no report of this has been made to the Ministry Dr Prescott. Nobody t-told me.'

She turns from Prescott and smiles at you, amused.

'Dear, oh dear. You've upset the little one Ernest. No, Jalovec, you haven't been notified of this simply because adamant Amherst dismissed the idea and conveniently lost those reports which we submitted on the subject. Don't let it upset you though, the rig is quite safe. Only now big Beattie, the rig boss, has sent a coded message to States-Lever saying that their precious three million pounds worth of oil rig is ready for the deep six. So when they confront the Minister with this news, his surprise will only be surpassed by his fury. I imagine.'

'And what is Sir Martin doing about that, Doctor?'

'The dear old gentleman is at the moment frantically typing out an emergency briefing to be radioed to his superiors, denying that the rig is in danger of even having work halted for a few hours never mind being brought down.'

'So the minister will dismiss States-Lever, and we'll be stuck out here after all.'

'Ah, the thought of working with us on this most challenging exciting project doesn't stimulate you then, Jalovec?'

'Oh ... no no, it isn't that at all Dr Daily ... '

'My, my, how you squirm, but don't worry. The Minister will crack. Won't he Ernest?'

'Well, er, yes. I think.'

'Of course he will you bevel brain. The oil company will rake up all it can find on the *Sea Gem* disaster for public support. Then they'll throw some nasty figures into Whitehall, like two hundred and fifty pounds per hour for stoppages, or about six thousand a day. Of course the loss of the rig would cost millions.

'No, I don't think the Minister will dismiss States-Lever at all. In fact I believe that the sea lily is in the last twenty-four hours of its illustrious mysterious existence.'

Prescott is looking at her, pained.

'But Fenella, that means that you and I will be split up, after all these weeks here, together ... '

'Mmm pity isn't it? Until that does happen though we may as well keep ourselves busy with some work. You go on reading through those reports Jalovec.'

See how she moves, like a lynx. Prescott is gaping at her, his eyes two burning studs embedded in his face, LUST stamped on his forehead in four inch high fluorescent lettering.

Down to the reports all of them reading like oriental riddles. Occasional saunters around the thirty foot square lab jammed to the ceiling with equipment. Microscope specimen slides, a three foot thick cross section of lily flesh, and alien cell cultures thriving in ammoniac solution, all to be studied. A puzzle furrow forming now between your close set eyes.

What have we here?

No iron?

Ridiculously high quantities of cobalt, of vanadium, of molybdenum, and all swimming around in gallons of propionic acid.

Throughout each of the lily's three leaves is spread a fine fibrous network. A nervous system? Who knows? Analysis shows weird carbon – carbon chains with fluorine in the side chains and reddish crystals of m-aminobenzoic acid. Plenty of electricity too: the output of a small power station. It must be a nervous system.

'A nervous system,' excitedly smacking right fist into left palm.

She looks up at you, all emerald eyes.

'I beg your pardon?' irritated.

'The network, couldn't it be some sort of nervous system?'

'I did think of that, Jalovec.' Bored already and turning back to the electron microscope.

'But did you test it out? Electric and chemical stimuli, noting any slight variations in current? Did you find out if there is any reaction to changes in light and temperature? Did you see if you could find any parallel between the nervous system of other creatures and the network in the lily? Did you search for possible nerve centres? Did you … '

'Yes, Jalovec.' Absorbed in her work.

'Oh.' Quietly.

Deflated you pick up the reports and try to read. Stop your eyes rolling away from the pages. Stop peeking at her legs. Stop your concentration from slacking. Your thoughts worm around to how soft she must be, how warm, smooth and sweet is her skin under that virginal white lab coat. What luxurious revels you and she

could have, listening to her whispering in your midnight ear, 'I'm
a woman. Be cruel to me ... '
— Control yourself
   Or finish up like pitiful Prescott,
   Ogling her
   Through a retort
   Steamed up from his openmouthed
   Breathing.
The door flies open letting the wind lift the papers from your
knee and flick them under a bench and beyond. You are scram-
bling in pursuit of them when someone comes in, walks across to
Fenella Daily, and begins talking to her in a deep rusty voice which
would be a boon to any rag and bone man.

When the door is eventually pushed closed by Prescott you
manage to recover all the wandering sheafs somewhat crumpled
and soiled. Standing up with them in your arms you are faced with
six foot of greasy industrial clothing impressively filled with
muscle, hair, and handsome features.

Straighten up to your full five foot one.

Look him straight in the eye.

'What's this?' asks the voice rumbling up from his knees if not
somewhere even lower.

'This, Mr Beattie, is my new assistant, Jalovec.'

'Another runt like Goodwin, only he had more on top.'

From Beattie's vantage point your balding spot is obviously
visible.

'You really have a kinky taste in assistants, Fenella sugar.'

Prescott chokes slightly.

'Kindly address Dr Daily by her proper title Beattie. Your
forwardness is becoming objectionable.'

'Screw yourself old fellow. Just give Amherst my message
when you see him like a good chap now. 'Evening gentlefolk.'

Another blast of sea air, the door slams, and he has gone.
Prescott stands looking after him, enraged, quivering like a badly
struck arrow.

'Excuse me Dr Prescott, what message was that?'

'Huh? Oh something about the r/t being on the blink.'

'R/t?'

'Radio telephone, idiot!' Fenella is snappy. Beattie apparently upsets her. Probably the only male who could have her anytime, and they both know it.

'Then we have no communication with the mainland at all now?'

'None, apart from the transistor set in the saloon, and it's always tuned to Radio Scotland.'

A fresh thought drops into your head, as delightful as a newly laid egg.

'Sir Martin's report can't go out then.'

'Remarkable observation, Jalovec. You may soon be as brilliant as bright Ernest here.' Smiling maliciously she takes off the lab coat to display sleek grey skirt and white sweater. Prescott's optics seem to pop like a couple of flash bulbs. He grins weakly as she combs her hair, moving her arms and neck sinuously.

'Well, Fenella, the old man's going to be in one terribly filthy mood when he finds out. I suggest that we all retire to our quarters as quickly as possible, and try to steer clear of his path tomorrow.'

'The essence of courage, aren't you my darling? Why look at the marvellous way that you faced up to big bad Beattie, heroic.' She stands before him, runs her hands slowly across his shoulders and speaks gently. 'Now you're not really afraid of Sir Martin are you? You're not really afraid of him putting a mark against your name so black that you'd never get another job, even as a lav attendant, hmmm?'

Laughing softly she moves her body against him, arms around his neck …

— He's drooling …

The door opens again and is hastily closed. Standing there, rainbeads on cheeks, and outrage glowing crimson from his ears, Sir Martin Amherst.

'Out of order. Out of bloody order!

'Lies, lies, lies; great greasy slug of a liar tells me that the radio equipment's on the bum. Wet nosed cretin of a radio operator. Oh

I could hear it all right, crackling away in there like a mentally deficient old hag, but would they let me near it? Not on your life. Damn all up with the thing and well I know it. "The drift of the lily will damage the rig within the next three days" if you please. The only drift that's going to do any damage around here'll be the drift of my boot into Beattie's backside as soon as I set eyes on him.'

He glances at you.

'And you, Javelin, or whatever you're called, I've written out a report on your disgraceful appearance this morning. There's another thing that the Minister is going to hear about. It had better not happen again.'

'No sir.'

'And you Prescott. I imagine this has been another of your incredibly fruitful days, unlocking the enigmas of the unknown by the hundredweight no doubt, shedding light in the biological darkness, striking an order in Chaos? Well, speak up man.'

A twitching smile on the victim's lips.

'Well, ha ha, you see, Sir Martin … '

'Oh yes I see. I see a damn sight better than you imagine. Stupidity, incompetence, and sloth. I picked you for my team on the strength of your work on *Idiacanthus Fasciola*. For a while I couldn't understand how such a magnificent thesis was principally the work of that undergraduate Briggs who died of leukemia out there in Mexico with your party.

'As soon as that r/t is operational I'm going to request an investigation into that rumour. There's something for you to sleep on Prescott.

'Goodnight Fenella my dear.'

'Goodnight Uncle Martin.'

— Uncle Martin!

The door bangs shut.

Prescott swings round and pulls you by the lapels to within inches of his bared brown teeth. He yells.

'Me. Why is it me he picks on?'

'It should be you; you with your ridiculous wog name. You, the snivelling stunted misfit, without breeding or even a proper education.

'And me; me with a public school, Oxford, first class honours, and doctorate. Do you hear that?

'Doctorate.'

His punch bounces you backwards off a steel cabinet and onto the floor. His voice softens to a cracked whisper.

'No sense of proportion, none.'

Fenella is back against the Stereoscan, her eyes alive with alarm and excitement. She laughs.

'Tut tut, Ernest don't upset yourself over the old horse. He's just angry with Beattie and looking for someone to take it out on. That's all. Anyway he's drunk.'

As you come to your feet Prescott hands you your coat with a mumbled apology. Dabbing at your bleeding lips with a slightly used handkerchief you push the daily reports into your brief case and step outside. Walk across the rig through the bustling busy dark, and then climb down the ladder into light and warmth. Strip your mac off, shake it roughly and start folding it up. Lucky for that big swine that you didn't use the fatal karate chop to the neck which you'd read about in that article in *Man*. Huh. If only he knew how close he came. Water flowing into eyes. Lump rising in throat. Self pity.

— Fight it.

What is keeping those two anyway? They should have come to the hatch by now. Wait another minute staring up the ladder at the square of black night. She was directly behind you. What are they doing up there? Grasping the handrails, placing your foot on the bottom rung you decide to climb up and peep over the edge. Then suddenly she is above you and descends straight into your arms. There is teasing delicate perfume from her hair and you find yourself nuzzling the nape of her neck, your arms encircling her waist.

She stiffens.

'Don't even think about it, Jalovec. Only Snow White goes in for dwarfs.'

You step back and she turns to face you, her eyes the deep green of arctic seas.

Prescott descends with heavy clumps, his lips still trembling from the Amherst fusillade, and stands clasping and unclasping his hands in anguish. Emotional development obviously arrested at the age of twelve. She links arms with him and mutters to you in a monotone.

'I trust you can find your own way back to your quarters.'

'Oh yes, er, thanks for showing me the reports and everything ...'

But already she is walking away with him, talking in a light mocking voice.

'You're frightened again Ernest? You'll need a spot of the Amherst brandy to help you sleep tonight.'

With ten minutes past you finally come to your cabin, enter, unpack the pin-up magazines, spread them out on your bed, and kneel. Commence weaving of fantasies, cruel fantasies tonight around the provocative positions of those glossy bodies, around bloated Amherst, leprous Prescott, and around her, especially around her.

But this is not escape enough. The twin pains of bruised lip and broken ego demand more. You lean over to your duffle bag and take out a compact leather case which unclips to reveal a small portable tape recorder complete with a spool ready for playback. You place the listening device in your ear and switch on. There is the naked hiss of unspoiled tape for a few seconds, followed by the rumpling sound of microphone being lifted. Then the female voice deep and vibrant.

'Darling, oh darling you're wonderful. There could never be anyone quite like you.' An actress, expensive but worth the money. *'There are such depths in you.'* Marvellous expression she has. *'You are so tender, my love, so different from the rest of men. They are all so coarse and insensitive compared with you.'* True, true, even if you did write the words yourself. *'You are the, the only man who really understands everything about* women. *You can make us do anything.'* And still studying the photographs of tempting looks, impassioned mouths. *'I need you, crave for you.*

Oh God do with me what you will ... '

Bang. Bang. Bang.

On the door.

'Open up. He's done it. The Minister's done it.'

Emergency dumping of mags and tape recorder under the bunk.

Jumping up you unlock the door.

Enter the villain giggling wildly. Prescott.

'He's done it Jalovec. Just heard it on the eleven o'clock news bulletin. The risk to the rig is too great, he says. So 'D' class destroyer *Deterrence* will arrive tomorrow at fifteen hundred hours to dispatch the hazard.'

He drops to the bed bawling lungfuls of laughter.

'And Amherst, you should have seen him ... going off like a roman candle ... face like peeled beetroot ... screaming at those greasy roughnecks in the saloon.'

Down on his knees now convulsing.

'He kept talking about ... about "prizeworthy research" ... that's what he was out here after ... a big plump Nobel ... and it's out the window now ... Funny, Jalovec. ... Funny ... '

Hysterics on the floor.

Kick him out.

Go to bed.

The black fluids of sleep.

You are drowning in them, gasping, choking, thrashing wild arms blindly.

Until you break the surface and lie there wet with sweat, bed blankets knotted at your feet.

A brutal headache is throbbing with the rhythm of your pulse beats, and you are shaking like a bad case of *delirium tremens*.

Glance at your watch.

Five o' clock.

Aye, what a collection of gruesome old nightmares that was. Probably just because you are sleeping in a strange bed. Have a walk around for a bit. That should freshen you up a shade. And a cold shower followed by a jaunt to the saloon for a cup of strong tea wouldn't be a bad idea either.

The freezing jet of water explodes across your face and chest as you vigorously rub hard fingers into your scalp. Nothing to touch a wet massage as a cure for headaches. Step shivering from the cubicle and pick up a towel for a brisk rub down.

The saloon is suprisingly crowded. Of course, the 'graveyard shift' will be coming off at six o' clock and the other crew will be going on for the next twelve hours. There are about twenty of them sitting at the tables. The white protective helmets lying beside food piled plates and coloured plastic mugs. Long blue threads of cigarette smoke coil up from overflowing ashtrays. Something is wrong.

The silence.

No one speaks.

Only the nagging rasp of a smoker's morning cough from the back of the room. Faces of clay with lifeless red-rimmed eyes, expressionless and unseeing. Riggers, wire-men, tool-pushers, all eating slowly thoughtlessly, not even looking at the meal before them.

    — They can't all be
    Hungover.
    Amherst's
    Is the only booze
    On board.

Big frown as you catch sight of Prescott's back where he is sitting over beside the still record player — with Beattie and Amherst. What are they doing in here at this time of the morning? Anyway you can always walk across to them and ask them what everybody is so depressed about today.

Smile heartily.

'Er, good morning, gentlemen, er … '

No response.

Beattie's nose is running but he does not seem to be aware of it, or of anything else.

You move back trembling slightly, worry and wonder breaking out in your mind. Tiny fears trickle down your back.

—Now don't panic
 Do something
 Constructive.

Yes, switch on the radio, but what station is broadcasting at half five. Too early? Try the 'Light' anyway.

' *... who was a defeated candidate in the French general elections of last December has died at the age of sixty-three in his villa outside Nice.'*

That's it, the news.

'The mysterious marine growth which appeared quite suddenly around the oil rig Sea Horse *a few months ago is to be destroyed this afternoon as the pull of the ocean currents on the growth is endangering the rig. A Royal Navy destroyer will take off the entire crew of* Sea Horse *and then dispatch the hazard using flame-throwing equipment.'*

A gutteral growling reverberates through the room, and you turn to see all eyes become bright and vicious staring at the radio.

Amherst and Prescott jump to their feet, spilling sugar, tea and salt cellar to the floor. Sir Martin wrenches the transistor set from your grasp and places it on a table while Prescott goes behind the counter and opens a small cupboard from which he lifts an old cleaning rag reeking of methylated spirits. He drapes this over the radio.

Sir Martin reaches out with his cigarette lighter.

The two men seated at the table gaze blankly ahead.

' *... and now it's time for breakfast special ... '*

Click.

Phoomff.

Very spectacular the way that those flames belch up ceiling high. Dramatic. Impressive.

— What in
 Hell is
 Going
 On?

The transistor collapses showering molten plastic and burning cloth across one of the roughnecks wearing only his mucky leather jacket over well slept pyjamas. He begins to scream.

You push Prescott aside, grab the fellow from behind and drag him away from fire. Drop him to the floor and douse his clothes with the contents of a quart bottle of milk.

Your cardigan sleeve has caught light. Rip the thing off and start beating it into the blaze. Kick the other roughneck away from the table, sending him sprawling against the door. Over there, above the cooker in the galley, a fire extinguisher.

Pull it from the wall.

How does the damn thing work?

Pull the pin and lift the funnel.

A thick foam fountain hits the burning mess and sprays out across the room, leaving the air heavy with smoke and fumes.

The fire is dead.

Coughing and retching, water streaming out of your eyes, you try to shout at them, but only a hoarse screech comes out.

'What's the game then, eh? What's the game? You could have killed us all. Bloody idiots. What are you all sitting there for like stuffed prunes, or something? Don't just gawk at me. For Christ's sake ....

'Prescott, Sir Martin, speak ....

'Have you all slipped your gears, or something?

'What's wrong?

'Am I dreaming? Is this a nightmare or something? Just another nightmare .... '

Stagger outside to where the noise of machinery and reality can be heard more clearly.

Machinery!

Then someone must be working. Someone must be sane somewhere.

You are running. Along corridors, through hatches, down ladders, across passages to the bottom of the rig, to the base of the derrick.

To the work box.

They are lifting the drill string, two miles or so of it, to replace the worn away bit. Men, grimy figures with safety hats and overalls and boots. But all moving with the dull efficiency of robotoids, all with the same dead countenances, all estranged from their actions.

Working with a fierce zeal they uncouple each thirty foot section of pipe as it comes up hot wreathed in steam, hose it down, grease the threads, and stack it. Rivulets of perspiration course down the temples into the ears and then drip onto the necks and shirts.

Mindless automatons.

You walk away.

Back to your cabin. That is the only escape. Go to sleep and reawaken. Yes, reawaken when the world has found its reason.

In your cabin you break open the large hamper of selected health foods which you brought from the mainland to ensure that you did not suffer from any dietary deficiency. Opening a can of blended vegetable juices you swallow it all in one draught.

Now just climb on top of the dishevelled bunk and lie down. Peace, sweet peace. Calm and then …

Asleep.

The alarm clock has just stopped ringing on the floor. Grunt and stick your head over the side to look at the time. Twenty to ten. Another interview with Sir Martin today at ten. Ah well better get up. Funny dream that was last night about the fire in the saloon and the rest of it. Funny.

Just a moment. You are lying in bed fully clothed and there is an empty can of vegetable juice on the floor.

Steady now, steady. Probably just couldn't sleep and went for a short stroll, worked up a thirst and had something to drink on returning. After all, it is sheer foolishness to even consider that such a weird fantasy could actually have taken place. After all.

But what if it did ….?

A loud lusty voice sings raucously past your door en route to the saloon, crushing the budding fears. Of course it was just another nightmare. Everyone turned into zombies, an interesting twist of the imagination, probably with some amusing Freudian significance.

Sounds of gaiety as you walk towards Amherst's office. Laughs, whistles, and shouts from the dormitory and washroom. While you think of what sweet words and tender phrases await your arrival at his door.

'Come in Jalovec. Come in my boy.'

Wide grin on him this morning. Maybe the Minister has decided not to destroy the sea lily after all. Stuck out here for months in that case; nauseating thought.

'Take a seat my lad. That's better now. Well I want you to know that I'm scrapping that silly report I was going to send in on your unfortunate appearance yesterday. Instead it will be replaced with my description of your bravery and split second speed in saving us when the radio went up in the saloon this morning. Damn good show.'

It happened. It really happened then.

'Fine performance you know. The true spirit of St George that you find in every thoroughbred Englishman.'

'Actually, sir, my parents are Czechs.'

'Well a drop of wog blood makes you cosmopolitan.'

'About that incident in the saloon, Sir Martin … '

'Selfless courage pure and simple. You're not even one of us and yet you risked life and limb in that fire. Highly commendable. Now if you'll run along I'll finish writing my little piece on Prescott. Disgusting the things that they are saying about the poor chap you know. Disgusting. But my report on him will soon put paid to all those smutty lies, you'll see. He's a fine upstanding fellow Prescott. Fine fellow.'

Backing slowly away from him, with your eyebrows raised, bemused.

'Oh yes, and Jalovec if you see Beattie tell him not to worry. If he doesn't want to send the message to States-Lever about saving the sea lily I quite understand. I know that it would probably weaken his position as a rig boss with the company. So I'll send the call out to the Ministry as soon as the r/t is functioning again.'

'Uh – Beattie and his men want to *save* the lily now?'

'Naturally.'

'Oh! er, of course Sir Martin. Good morning.'

' Morning.'

There is a foul smell about this whole carry on and it is not from
your bad breath. You close the door behind you and make your
way to the lab shack. Turn the handle. Locked. Give the customary
few knocks and a couple of shouts.

'Anyone in? Dr Daily? Prescott?'

Start kicking, but not too hard. Shoe-leather is expensive these
days. No luck. Shrug and walk off. Where is everybody and what
is happening around here? Is Amherst schizophrenic? It's probable enough.

The day shift are carrying on with the job of pulling up the drill
pipe, but with more vigour and expression than the other crew. No
clockwork motions here but smooth action and perfect teamwork.
One of the tool-pushers glances up at you and casually waves a
gloved hand before returning to the work in hand.

An amorphous discomfort hangs about you. Why did he do
that? Nobody ever waved at you before. Puzzled you wander off
to the saloon hoping to find some company. But it is empty.

The charred table has been broken up and the remains stacked
neatly behind the counter.

Laughter, and songs.

It is coming from outside. You step out onto the catwalk and
freeze in disbelief. There is no liquor permitted on the rig for crew
consumption, but before you are about two dozen men swaying
around obviously falling-down-drunk and singing the praises of
'Plymouth Nell,' 'The house of seven doors,' together with other
off-key ditties. Leaning against the wall, and each other, for
support are Prescott and Beattie.

—Perhaps all this
   is merely but
   Another
   Dream.

First Amherst gone amicable, now Prescott and Beattie. Top
with a rich layer of drunken roustabouts who have not been near

the hard stuff for days, and what do you have?

Nutcake.

'Hey there, Jalovec.'

Prescott bounds over and grasps you by the hand.

Beattie is shouting to the men.

'Here he is lads.'

And up go their cheers, sincere, loud and good humoured.

Then you are in their fumbling tugging grasp, pulling you disconcertingly nearer the siderail. A tall derrick-hand with garish ginger beard and commanding eyes catches you by the shoulder. He shouts.

'Get an eyeful of that down there me old son and tell us what you think of it. That's our lily.'

That down there.

With the intricate extravagance of a frost fantasia on a winter window, crystalline colours aglitter under the chill bright sun, and fluctuating like wind waves on wheatfields, the sea lily.

Lying down there. Arrogant in its coarse splendour.

That down there.

Nibbling at your lower lip you push your way over to the door and leave them.

No longer perplexed.

But frightened.

Again.

To bed. The only place to be at such times as this. Pass the radio room where the quarz-faced youth is bending over the spark popping equipment. Tears of fat frustration as he mutters to himself.

'Won't go. Dammit.

'Won't go.'

Scuttle away down the corridors. Until you hurriedly go past a figure in pink and halt two yards further on. Turn slowly around. She stands in front of the generator room door. Flamingo slacks and blouse. Very becoming. But the face …

Smiling.

'Hello.'

'Dr Daily I ... '

'Fenella. Call me Fenella.'

'Well, er, Fenella ... '

She springs over to you, puts slender hands behind your head, draws it to her. And rubs noses.

'I like the way you say my name. Say it again.'

   — Proverbial last straw.

     Swallow very hard.

     Jump back.

     Run.

'Fear of the unknown.' An expression which you have used often in mocking the ignorant. Here you sit scared sick, making a midday snack of your finger-nails. Try a little self analysis. First of all, do you feel ill? Yes. Hmm, and you feel apprehensive about the state of things? Very definitely. Well then which change upsets you more, the personality transformations in the people around you, or the alteration of the sea lily from scummy green to startling gaudiness? The people upset me — they despised me yesterday — ignored me and everything else this morning — and now they seem to *like* me. It's positively unnatural. Nobody ever takes to me. Perhaps what changed the sea lily changed everyone's personalities as well. Aha, there's a thought ....

An insane extrovert sprays the lily with some new type of luminescent paints and then runs around dropping soluble hypnotic tablets in the tea, coffee, soup etc., but none of these entered your body as you have your own food supply, three months of it, together with tinned milk and other highly nutrient beverages. Prescott's behind it all. A spy from some oil company which wants the secrets of States-Lever's sea drilling techniques.

Nok. Nok.

Someone at the door.

Prescott come to finish you off?

Remember lethal karate blow to neck. OK ....

'Whooss, herrromf .... *who is there?*'

Be calm. Confidence is the key.

Nok. Nok. Nokkety nok.

'Can I come in Jalovec?'

Fenella's voice.

'All right. The door isn't locked.'

She steps in still smiling.

'What are you doing in here, darling, all alone? Come out and look at the lily with me.' Softly.

'Thank you, but I am feeling a fraction off key today and I'd much rather go to my bed at the moment.'

'Lovely.'

She is unbuttoning her blouse.

'Uuuh?'

'I'll come in beside you and make you all warm and snug,' as the blouse drops and she reaches for the zipper on her slacks.

' … what? … '

And your heart goes bouncey bouncey bouncey against your rib cage.

'*No*,' with a twitching shake of your head. 'No n-no. Out out. *Out.*'

Pushing her, blouse, and hurt expression into the corridor.

'But Jalovec …. '

Slam the door. Double lock. Haul the desk over against it. Mustn't panic now lad. Keep a grip on yourself. Into bed. Into bed. Off with shoes, socks, and everything down to your woollen undies. Pull back the sheets and dive in. Move about until it is warm. Curl up into a ball. Bury your face in the pillow. Imagine you are about four years old again. Life is good. Life is simple. Dad gives you sixpence for running down with his line to the bookie's. Mum gives you a slap across the bum for starting a fire in a dustbin when her washing is out to dry. Those were the days.

'Jalovec,' through the keyhole.

'Go 'way.'

'Jalovec it's me.'

'Who's *me?*'

'Brian. Brian Beattie.'

'What do you want Beattie. I'm ill.'

'I thought that maybe you'd like to swap cabins with me. You must have nothing but the best from now on you know.'

Sounds appetising.

Out of bed, move the barricade, open the door and poke your head round.

'Seems a very reasonable proposition to me Brian.'

'Good. I've brought along a couple of roughnecks to move your gear along.'

'Just a minute then.'

Reach under the bunk for pin-ups and tape recorder. Toss them into the duffle.

'OK, come in now.'

Enter three colossal grotesques grinning obsequiously. Beattie shoulders your enormous food hamper. The other two lift the suit cases and duffle bag then follow their boss out along the corridor. Carrying your bundle of clothes and at the same time in the act of pulling on your trousers, you hop along behind them.

— Ready

To burst

Into songs.

Beattie's apartment is comparatively palatial, furnished with large double bed, plush settee with plush armchairs to match, electric 'coal' effect fire. And Amherst's is not the only booze aboard after all. Beside that elegant bed, an elegant table stacked with drink.

Step inside. Even a carpet on the floor.

The men leave your bags down beside the wardrobe and Beattie comes over to you, claps you on the back.

'That was a brave thing you done lad,' his earthquake of a voice grinding with emotion, 'and don't think that'll be forgotten in a hurry. It won't.'

They walk out.

Great fuss they are making over that fire. Odd. But might as well play along with the 'hero' tag while it sticks to you. Leap onto the new bed. The sumptuous mattress almost swallows you alive. Who would ever have thought Beattie to be so sensual? Ah, at the foot of the bed, hanging on the wall, a life-size painting of a beautiful blonde girl, reclining, sultry, nude. Mmmm.

Oh yes, yes, very homelike indeed.

Drrring, drrring.

'Who, uh?'

On the table. Hidden by a battery of bottles.

Λ telephone.

'Hello, er, Jalovec speaking.'

'You must help us.' Sir Martin's voice. 'We didn't manage to repair the r/t and they've arrived.'

'Wha ....?'

'The Navy, Jalovec they've arrived. You know, the destroyer that's supposed to kill the lily.'

'Oh yes?'

'You'll have to come and speak to them. I ... I can't face them Jalovec. They're sending someone across just now. Could you come and speak to him?'

'Well if you think that I can help ... '

'I'm sure you could persuade him to leave it alone Jalovec. The men will be in the saloon waiting to hear how you fare. I'll meet you on the lower catwalk in five minutes then.'

'All right. Goodbye.'

'Goodbye.'

On with your best terylene tie. Plaster down your thinning hair against the head, using rose-water from a cabinet in the toilet. Beattie is full of little surprises. Scrutinise yourself in the mirror and try knitting your brows. Very officious. Pity your eyes are so close set.

Outside the winds have abated and Amherst, Prescott, and Beattie await. Way down on the sea a small power boat from the grey sleek mass of the fighting ship. It draws alongside the far fringe of the lily and discharges a figure. A man, walking towards you, staggering occasionally across the vivid whorls of peregrine flesh.

Up he climbs, the fifty foot of a ladder to the top where exhaustion lies ruddy on his face.

'How do you do gentlemen. I am Captain Loewe,' puffing.

A bunch of how-do-you-do's in reply.

He smiles. Real dazzlers those teeth. And all together very distinguished. Greying hair even. He is actually Beattie's peer in height. Wow!

'I'd like to discuss the evacuation of the rig with you. Like to get it moving as soon as you can manage. Must be ready for the big show at three o'clock you know. There'll be a good deal of news coverage you realise; couple of small ships and some aircraft I believe. Must be ready.'

'You'd had better speak to Mr Jalovec about that. He's in charge here now.' Amherst's voice is cracked.

'Who?' The captain gapes confusedly after the retreating trio.

'Me, captain.'

— Breathe in
   Look imposing.

'I'm afraid my instructions specify that I speak with Mr Beattie and Sir Martin Amherst. They don't mention anyone called Jarevec … '

He is trying to dominate you. Use desperate methods.

'Now here this sailor. I'm the cheese around this village, like grampa says, so if you want to gas off do it now, if not you can start swimming back to your little tin boat, and go on playing admirals,' all in the best Mickey Spillane phraseology.

'Eh?'

'See kiddo. Like us guys have just arrived at something big on the science scene with the funny flower down there but we've been in a fix over it since our noodlehead radio operator blew the ass out of the r/t. So all I want from you is a jaw with the big boys at the Ministry, over your yak box. Then you can go on home. You won't be needed. Clear?'

'I would like to know exactly by what authority you … '

'Do your ears need cleaning, punk? I got real strong pals sitting on plenty power which they'll swing when I whistle, so don't pull the bull on me, or you'll find you've gotten it pushed up your tail.'

Frightfully eloquent, what?

'This is somewhat unorthodox, but I can accommodate you as far as the radio goes. However if I am advised to complete my mission I shall proceed to destroy the growth whether or not evacuation … has … *aah.*'

He folds up and flops down. Flecks of froth from the mouth, groaning.

Dear damn I swear I never touched him.

Foetus position now, eyeballs rolling up.

Don't flee. A drop of courage, just this once, for only a moment. Please.

Kneel beside him. *Kneel!* That's better. Now, unbutton his jacket, and loosen his tie, and open his collar.

The groans diminish gradually until he is lying still, looking through the rails at the lily.

'I won't,' hoarse and panting.

'Beg your pardon, sir?'

'Won't harm a tissue of it, Jalovec. I won't take the ship near it. Honest.' Standing up now but a trifle unsteady.

'That's really very decent of you, captain.'

What is wrong with his eyes? They look as if they have been pickled.

'Listen to it. Makes me feel good to listen to all that happiness.'

Listen to what? Is he mirawkulous? An ebriose captain on your hands?

'Feeling odd?'

'Feeling marvellous, and I'll tell you if you were in the Royal Navy I'd personally have seen to it that you received a commendation for your action in the saloon this morning. At least a commendation.'

'Oh? … Hey, how did you find out about that?'

Big smile, quite sober now.

'Can't you guess?'

Bewildered by the entire episode you shake your head.

Still smiling he tidies up his appearance. Then with complete aplomb swings onto the ladder and descends from view.

Stupefied you walk into the saloon to be greeted by cheering, roistering, and general frivolities. Amherst standing on the counter, a mug of cocoa in his fist, the frown of worry tossed away like so many old paper handkerchiefs.

'For he's a jolly good fellow, etc,' bursting out at the sight of you.

Shouts about 'Jalovec the Lily-Saviour.'

But you have not had time to tell them. How did they find out? It's not as if they are mind readers or psychic or … What if they are?

Psychic.

Telepaths maybe, eh?

Naaaww ridiculous. Why all they have in common with one another is the fact that they work here on *Sea Horse*. There are Geordie wiremen, Irish and Scottish drill men, a Texan geologist, a Welsh electrician among the assortment of nationalities and skills employed on the rig. Even a knight. Absolutely nothing in common.

Except the lily. The sea lily.

That is it. The unknown potential amongst the known. The incalculable factor. Now if it is telepathic events then take on a different aspect. Obviously it's not too smart. No measurable intelligence at all in fact. So this takeover of the minds around you is an instinctive reaction, like the chameleon changing its colour.

Lily did that as well coming to think of it.

Some kind of survival mechanism.

Telepathic, then it can pick up hostile thoughts, and when they are strong, threatening destruction, like last night, like the captain's, it averts its own annihilation by turning these thoughts to ones of love.

Don't think like that. It's scarey.

All of these ebullient men actually in an induced love trance. Agents of the unknown, no less.

Dropping the fat ham sandwich just pushed into your hand by a grinning tool-pusher you scamper off like a well kicked cur.

During your flight from the saloon you change direction twice, firstly because in your panic you lose yourself and the second time because you remember that you no longer live in the midget bedroom but in the grand master suite. Approaching the great solid door with growing sensations of security. You're just going to stay in here until they send you back to dry land. To Hell with research. The whole place is crawling with head cases.

Step into the cabin.

No escape.

Prescott and Fenella are sitting on the settee. What are they doing here? Are they in the mind grip of the sea lily? Oh yes, from the way they've been acting they must be. Perhaps the lily has no longer any use for you. After all you seem to be the only person unaffected by its power. Are they here to finish you off?

Prescott speaks.

'Hello Jalovec. That was good work on Captain Loewe, old chap. Champion.'

But now it is time for the big pay-off. Is that what you mean?

Your eyes widen, breathing becomes spasmodic, shivering, hot and cold bursts of sweating. Go to it bravely. A touch of the carefree panaches.

Say something, gay.

' … hello … '

'Hello darling.'

Oh that voice does disreputable things to your metabolism. Something starts sniggering down evilly deep in your dark insides.

'Do you two want me for anything in … particular?'

They nod.

Another blast of the shakes. Teeth achatter.

'It's about myself and Fenella, Jalovec.' He stands up. 'We were unofficially engaged. Honeymoon on my father's Jamaica estate. Tobacco plantations you know. Lovely view of the Blue Mountains too. Ah well, that's life.

'You see she has told me that it is you whom she loves. I must say however that I cannot blame her. I can tell when I'm beaten. When one realises that one's rival is not only the best man for the girl, but also the very friend who saved one's life in an act of selfless courage, what can one do but shake on it and retire gracefully?'

He sticks out a nicotine browned hand.

A brief but hearty handshake and he walks out, a generous smile of self-sacrifice on his lips.

'That just leaves you and I,' tingling words.

' "You and me" is actually the correct grammatical form, Fenella,' and a snappy census of the room proves her statement to be correct.

'That is what I mean.' Hair a sweeping cascade of flaring inferno. She moves over to where you are standing, in the far corner.

'The Navy. They're not going to … to … ' your voice shooting up to a squeak.

'I know, Jalovec, I know.' Her arms around your neck.

'How do you know? How can you possibly know, any of you?' in a croaky contralto.

'Can't you guess?' Laughing, she draws herself against you.

— *Yipeeee*. It's Xmas.

It is only afterwards, with her rich red hair on the pillow, that you decide to donate the large painting of the nude to the saloon, and, while the mood is on you, why not rig up the ego-inflating tape recorder in the dormitory? After all who wants the wrapper when you can have the loaf inside? And what swinging bread.

Lying there thinking about the lily and the fascinating reversal of polarities in your relations with society. People praising you, smiling, idolising and even sleeping with you. Love, funny stuff. They actually love you. All of them. You tremble, push your face down to the delicate warmth of her throat for comfort, for sanctuary; for you are a man too long disprized.

Now consider the sea lily.

It has tied everyone here together with some strong and undoubtedly emotional bonds. On the conscious level they all seem to separate individuals but what about the deeper levels of their minds? A communal subconscious, perhaps?

Yes there is a possibility. They are aware of what is happening in that case, but not completely, just enough for them to consent to it. Certainly you have not seen anyone fighting the influence.

Destruction of all aggression, or at least all antisocial aggression, and not just that which is hostile to the lily itself.

Very nice.

When you walked into the saloon this morning no one was completely readjusted. All minds in a mental vortex. The radio emitted hostility. They decided to give a dose of what their fuzzy brains believed was its own medicine.

They 'killed' the radio.

And almost included themselves in the deal at the same time. That accounts for the big gratitude for you stepping in, because if their survival instinct is one with the lily's then the saving of the two roughnecks from the fire had the same effect of saving every one of them and the lily itself.

But that does not explain why the growth did a Cinderella in reverse last night, from a scum-covered mush to that fascinating optical beanfeast. Think on it. Remember how all the crew who were not working were hanging drunk over the catwalks admiring 'their beautiful lily.'

Well maybe that colouring has some hypnotic effect? Perhaps.

Or perhaps it is subtler than that; they are now emotionally bound up with the lily, It has become part of their personalities, not a very attractive ingredient as a slimy greenish horror, but as an exotic blossom it gains their admiration. Yes, of course. It strengthens the tie through making the person admire it as a part of himself. Personal vanity. The old Narcissus weakness.

Oh, real sneaky, real dirty.

Fenella makes a small animalish sound and curls up to you. Snug as she would say.

The helicopters full of newsmen and cameras have returned long past to the mainland. But the three small craft which came out to cover the story of the lily's end are still with the destroyer. For about two hours this afternoon they lay waiting with the warship's guns trained on them while the telepathic net engulfed all the minds on board. Only one gentleman was similar to yourself in that he was immune, but your differences are more impressive than your semblances; he's in irons while you're in clover.

With HMS *Deterrence* on the doorstep the world is temporarily rosy, but do not delude yourself. No matter what excuses Captain Loewe has been fobbing off on Admiralty, Ministry, and sundry other authorities he cannot hold them at bay indefinitely. They are going to jump into the play-pit soon enough to see just what everyone's about.

You start to dress and worry.

There is an entire nation a mere one hundred miles away wondering just what in Hell is the game out here. Buttoning your duffle coat and pulling the hood up around your head. Along the sleeping corridors. Grit your teeth and step out into the scything night air. Could the lily cope with, what is it, about fifty million odd minds? Doubtful.

What is that?

Up there.

Among the glow-fringed blocks of black cloud the red-green-green-red-green of aircraft. Then up pops the big cold moon. Four of them. Sound like Shackletons. Change in engine pitch as one of the planes breaks formation and comes in low across the path of white sparkled water. Yes definitely Shackletons. The others are swinging down to follow him. Bizarre droning bugs they are. Louder, nearer, nearer. Hope they can see the rig because they're coming straight at you. Heh, heh.

Coming ... straight ... at ... *you.*

The one in front is almost on you.

Unswerving. Blind twit.

He's going to ...

'*Pullup Pullup. No nooo ...*'

Your yell is squandered in the Thunderblast of engines. The shape is gone, whipped overhead.

KRAAK!

A hard blue flare splutters up yonder. Below there is the

shimmering lily. Rising from its surface in slow undulation are thousands of fine pastel coloured fronds, slender, graceful; leaning out to the west, out against the flow of stiff northern wind.

Out to where Britain sleeps, tonight.

A sudden silence.

Startled, you sit erect in your bed.

It has stopped. The drilling has stopped. For two months you have been living with the noise, always some kind of noise. Even when they are changing the bit you hear the winches dragging up the long drill stem piece by piece. The inescapable rumble rumble creeping in everywhere with neither respect for any man nor respect for any occasion. But particularly diabolical in the lavs: it seems to echo through the plumbing and then vibrate up right into your very bowels. Nobody on Sea Horse has constipation.

Bang. Bang.

You jump.

'Come in, please.'

A laughing Brian Beattie pushes the door aside with a greasy protective glove.

'We've struck it. Natural gas.'

'My God. Really?'

'And the pressure's terrific. We're just about to ignite it. Coming to see?'

'Oh boy, oh boy, I'm coming. Ha ha hee. Sling me jacket on.'

Trotting eagerly behind the large man. Rapid happy voices abound, grinning faces, rowdy songs all round.

POOOOmm.

'YeeeeHaaaa.' Screaming cries seem to permeate the universe. You cringe uncontrollably.

'That'll be the men lighting the jet now.'

'Oh.' Straighten up and climb the ladder.

Great long twisting banner of flame writhing in the breeze. An assortment of toots, hoots, whistles, siren yells and other nautical music issues from the fourteen Royal Navy vessels at anchor round the rig.

Everyone is waving. Everyone is cheering.

Everyone is going to be rotten drunk tonight.

Amherst is smiling his superior smile. He appears to have lost a few morsels of the common altruism. Could his subconscious be trying to opt out of the love-tie? Probably. Jealousy most likely. He sees that you have all the say, all the power, and underneath it all he can't take it. He is greedy. But it will take years for the subliminal envy to wear him away to his old bureaucratic self. Seeing you looking at him he comes over, cups his hand to your ear, leans over and shouts.

'I see that you are not so easily impressed as these fellows, Jalovec. Look at Beattie over there, God bless him. He thinks this is November fifth. Or what about Prescott, from the way that he is gawking I'd say he's trying to work out how many refills for his gas lighter he'll get out of this lot.'

Nod and walk away.

Fenella is shouting something indistinguishable. Grasps you by the hand and starts to dance around laughing tempestuously. Soon the idea catches hold and a long chain of human hulks some in overalls others in pyjamas are doing the hokey kokey round the derrick. But used to a recent life of luxurious indulgence the pace soon becomes too strenuous for you. Legs throbbing angrily you totter delighted into your cabin, and sit gasping enthusiastically on the arm of a chair.

Uncap another bottle of whisky, and pour yourself one little nip. You tried to consume it in masculine mouthfuls until your five-day stint of the quaking purgatories which you passed almost entirely in the lav. Now you drink in moderation from a miniature crystal goblet so small that it would take over an hour to demolish at the rate of one glass per minute. Anyway you don't need it. If you need anything now it is Fenella.

Fecund Fenella Daily. The love-tie's most practical expression of its gratitude and love for you.

Your name is known to every person in the British Isles. The hero. Bringer of love. Jalovec.

Swallow the whisky.

Jalovec.

'I look in the mirror,
And what do I see?
The squat hairy goblin
That people call me.'

'Don't keep repeating that silly rhyme.'

Whirl about sending the goblet bouncing off of the deep pile carpet. Standing behind you at the record player she is turning the 'on' switch.

'You aren't like that at all. Maybe you are small but ... well you're the cuddliest man I know. So there.'

— A most singular compliment.

Out comes the music. 'Everybody loves a lover' Fenella's little joke. Almost the entire population of the British Isles are 'lovers' under the influence of the Lily. The very small number of exceptions. Estimated at about twelve hundred. They are mostly in hospitals undergoing hypnotic and drug treatments to break down their resistance. But there are a few who escape notice. The majority of these people are actually beneficial to the general condition. The balance of nature, or something to ensure that the healthy survive, or something. Because these free minds supply a more unbiased viewpoint on the 'amorous society' which cannot view itself objectively. The only danger lies in the hostile ones. Those immunes who hate the state of things which has ruined them financially or socially, or both.

Like that joker who boarded a hoverbus for pilgrims coming out for a trip around the Lily. Once inside the ring of guarding warships he pulled his haversack on to his back climbed out onto the roof, and jammed the hatch with a long steel nail shoved into one of the hinges. Lying flat on his belly he quickly set up an anti-tank rifle piecemeal from the bag. Rifle huh! The fellow blasted about fifteen craters in the flesh before the craft drew away far enough to be out of range. Then a rather distraught group of fellow passengers, who were mostly ladies, managed to open the hatch, and administered a spontaneous form of justice by lowering the screaming culprit down the wide funnel into the hover blades.

And that weapon was manufactured in the U.S. of A.

Sticky point is international relations. None of the British ambassadors abroad come under the love-tie. Each country has its own excuses for cutting links with the UK and Eire, but only a few specify the Lily. Most governments don't like to admit that the creature exists. However a handful of nations do have some considerable concern as regards the matter. Aerial photographs must certainly show the swollen seed pouches almost ready to burst open, and the idea of this does not help the sleep of government officials in those European states on the Atlantic seaboard. When all those cute little seeds go popping across the North Sea ....

Well look at Britain.

The party system of government has virtually collapsed with all sides putting forward motions and everyone supporting everyone else.

A horror of communalism. Anarchism even.

What a way to run a country.

And what a country.

Religion is raging like some plague of the conscience, even although all the Roman Catholics are in imminent danger of excommunication. The cries from the Vatican go completely unheard, or are disregarded, or are simply laughed at. After all how could so much love be 'the ultimate undermining force of the Devil and his legions'? Church unity has been overleaping all the old restraints. Everything in the evangelical garden is lovely.

Elsewhere in the country there have been more traumatic effects. Industrial relations have never been as good. Too good. The disappearance of almost all absenteeism, the boost in production figures, the cancelling of all strikes due to union demands being promptly met, competitive spirits virtually vanishing. The economy is doing pretty cartwheels. And collapsing. How could it be expected to survive?

The number of pregnancies both in and out of wedlock took a hysterical jump a couple of weeks ago.

Neither must one forget the desperate opening of thousands of clinics to contain the incredible spread of venereal diseases. But then what about the Amazing Disappearing Crime-wave. No criminals. Policemen out of work. And judges. And court officials. And prison personnel. And manufacturers of safes, burglar alarms, and all other security devices, hundred of firms of locksmiths. And companies supplying security transportation for shipments of money or valuables. Security is right out of fashion.

No exports either since the rest of the world stopped trading with Britain. No one sails, flies, or even tries a cross channel to the UK. There are aircraft belonging to British air companies in almost every international airport on the globe. The pilots and crew have simply broken contract, refused to return, and taken up flying these planes for other companies 'until such time as the situation is returned "to normal" '. Same goes for ships flying the Red Ensign. Right sickening isn't it? You'd expect some degree of loyalty from them. They'd just better keep out of gun range that's all.

The whole nation is only about a week away from social, political, and economic disintegration. And each one of Her Majesty's subjects not to mention the Irish are loving it.

Literally.

Not to worry.

The seed pouches will split tomorrow and then …. Well if the seeds grow as quickly as the Lily did, almost overnight, love will crush away all the nasty little hates and fears in millions of continental minds well within the week. Then things should brighten considerably. In the meantime nobody is starving.

But you are rather peckish.

Time for grub.

Off to the saloon with Fenella, hand in hand of course, to review today's menu.

MONDAY 19TH DECEMBER.

Cod, fried in vegetable oil, or boiled
Raw carrots, tomatoes, fresh peas,
Grated heart of lettuce.
Assorted cheeses.
Selection of nuts.
Whole wheat bread with butter.
Cocoa, hot chocolate, Bovril, Ovaltine, tea.
Tomorrow: Egg steaks.

NO SMOKING PLEASE.

Ah, delicious. What nutritional value. It was a wise decision to order nothing but health foods for the men, and how eagerly they have taken to them. No excess fat on their bodies these days. Why some of them are positively slim. Of course they spend one week in three back home and poison their systems with rubbishy meals. It is up to you to see that they are properly fed out here to compensate.

As you eat you hear the approaching rattle of a helicopter.

Funny.

The 'copter left at noon, just before you awoke. Perhaps it didn't arrive this morning and you were not informed. Funny.

Picking up a nine-inch-long carrot you bite a chunk out of it and rise from the table.

Fenella looks up from her plate.

'I'm just away out to see who the new arrivals are love.'

She nods approvingly and returns to the task of stuffing her mouth with boiled cod, big white steamy lumps of it. She is definitely becoming slimmer as well. Except for that slight swelling of her abdomen. Maybe, well … a baby? Mmm that would be nice.

It is colder. A fierce wind is churning distant waves against the now vast kaleidoscopic Lily. Walk shivering towards the landing plate.

As you reach the ladder she steps down all browns and reds

from the distorted plum shape of the setting sun.

'Mr Jalovec.' Statement not question.

'Who are you?'

Calm now lad she's only a woman.

'My name is Therese Spinks. How do you do?'

Shake the scented soft gloved hand.

'What did you say your name was?'

'Spinks, Therese, Miss.'

Ah well, we all have a cross to bear.

'Should I be expecting you for something or other Miss Spinks?'

'I can quite understand your bewilderment Mr Jalovec. I've arrived far too early. You see I'm here to interview you for *Madame.*'

'Oh, er, Madame who?'

'Ho, ho, I mean the magazine.'

'*Madame.* I've never heard of it.'

'But then you can hardly be expected to read popular female literature, Mr Jalovec.

'Anyway I'm about two hours early. You shall probably be notified of my visit in about half an hour. We, that is my editor, applied for permission to have an interview with you and it was granted, but the only helicopter which we could find on charter could not fly us out tomorrow due to commitment, and Wednesday would be far too late.

'So here I am,' defiantly.

'Pretty, isn't she?'

'Yes.'

'They said that you wouldn't mind being interviewed. After all, you are a National Figure.' She says it with capitals.

And you are.

'Come on down to my room then. We'll have a glass of something while we chat.'

'Thank you. That would be very nice.'

In the light of the flaring gas jet she looks Amazonian. Striding alongside you, black hair loose in the wind, dark eyes with sweet sumptuous centres.

You meet Prescott.

'Hello Ernest. This is Miss Spinks. She has come to interview me. This is Dr Prescott, Miss Spinks.'

'Very pleased to meet you Miss Spinks,' eagerly. His cheek is twitching nervously. Obscene, this man's reaction to women, any women. Really must see the doctor about him. It's getting desperate.

'Will you be coming to the party in the saloon tonight? I'll tell you what, after you've finished with Jalovec come along to my cabin and I'll tell you about the fascinating research I'm doing on the Lily and then .... '

'Thank you, Mr Prescott, but my magazine is *Madame* not *Biometrical Journal.* Good evening,' cutting him coldly down in mid-flight.

'Bu ... but ... '

And you are gone round a corner of the corridor into your room.

'Well, well I did not expect you to be living in such comfort.'

'Oh it satisfies my meagre requirements.'

Sitting down in an armchair she places her bulky leather shoulder bag at her feet and draws from it a cream coloured notebook.

'Shall we begin now?' smiling up at you and crossing her long legs. From where you stand, by the booze table, you have just been given a most appetising view of her lower thighs. Just a few tasty inches but enough to start the mild wrecking operations on your inhibitions. This should happen with Fenella.

'Er, herrrum. Well, yes, what would you like to know to start off with?' Your mouth is drying.

Need a drink.

Do something to keep your mind off those legs or you might do something regrettable.

'Where were you born?' still smiling. Couple of neat gold fillings in that mouth.

'Oh in Glasgow.' Look straight into her eyes and fight it.

'Dennistoun Maternity Hospital, to be exact.' You pour her a drink and bring it across.

'February second 1940,' holding the glass out. She reaches for it, her hand closing over yours.

'It was a Thursday.'

You lean closer to the promising perfumes.

Bash bash bash. That's your pulse.

'Two o'clock in ... the ... afternoon.'

Kiss.

Your fingers fumble for the phone and finally find it.

'This er, this is J-Jalovec. Um see that I'm not disturbed for the next ... herrum, next hour, or so.'

Slam the receiver down.

Lift all one hundred and forty pounds of her, and gasping hoarsely stagger across the room.

Great tumble into the bed.

'Oh please be gentle with me Jalovec, please. Oh Jalovec ... '

And so ... about thirty minutes later you are thinking. Nothing else your exhausted frame is capable of doing. Extraordinary how she has managed to keep that fabulous tan. All over. And at this time of year too without being able to so much as nip down to the Canaries some weekend for a quick bake on the beach.

Incredible.

Wham!

The shock leaves you paralytic.

Into the room comes a ferocious Fenella.

'What in Hell's going on then?'

'UGgg ggug gg .... '

'Get her *out*.'

'P-please Fenella. You're shouting. The whole rig can hear you.'

'I don't give a damn. *Out* with her.'

This is wrong. What about the love-tie?

Therese bounds from the bed, amazingly sprightly all things considered, and swings a cruel blow with the edge of her hand to Fenella's neck. The karate chop. Your red-haired Valkyrie crumples to the floor knocking over the bulky leather shoulder-bag which thuds open. To reveal wiring, transistors, and other suspicious little electronic trinkets.

You walk across. Kneel beside the unconscious form of Fenella and stare in disbelief at the compact but powerful transmitter.

'Methinks Miss Spinks stinks,' turning your head to look at her. She is sitting on the bed, legs crossed again, right arm resting on her knee, and in her hand something black pointed at your chest.

A gun.

'Sit still, or I will have the satisfaction of putting three bullets into your heart.'

— Thick heavy dread
    Like diesel oil
    Pours into your
    Guts.

'Oh no. No please don't do that … Don't hurt me, please.'

Another whining joins your own.

A sigh from her. Of relief?

There goes a high-pitched howl, probably one of the naval vessels. Then a distinct explosion. And another one, nearer.

'Telephone,' she points to the instrument, and then you realize that it has been ringing for almost a minute.

'Be careful what you say.'

You lift the receiver.

'Hello.'

'Jalovec?' Beattie's voice charged with panic. 'We're being attacked by aircraft. You must help us. There's some sort of jamming signal throwing all of the naval tracking equipment. We're helpless. Even our air cover is being affected by it. What do we do Jalovec? What do we do? Help us … '

You let it drop.

It swings from side to side, pathetically, a miniature voice pleading and sobbing from the earpiece.

Fenella grunts quietly on the floor.

More explosions, but still in the distance.

Suddenly the door flies open and Prescott is running over to you babbling and throwing his hands in the air.

'Been looking all over for you. Must take you and Miss Spinks to safety. There's a motor launch down … ' running flat when he first takes in her nakedness and then her pistol.

She points it at him.

'On your knees Prescott, quickly.'

But he doesn't.

Eyes wide he flings himself at her. Demented with lust and hate.

Bang, bang.

The two shots a couple of holes in the polished pine wardrobe. Twisting bundle of various arms and legs among the bedclothes.

Grab a bottle.

Walk over to the human octopoid, reach in, grip her hair and start pulling her head forward. Forward and down.

Down with the bottle hard behind the left ear twice. Second time it smashes, scattering whisky and shards of glass over the sheets. Prescott loosens his tie gasping for breath, and turns her round to look at her face.

A small drop of blood falls from her nose to spot the pillow. Eyes cold, accusing, glazing ….

He looks at you, amazed.

'Dead …. Jalovec.'

Boom boom boom.

Boom.

BAAANG!

The violence of the explosion rocks you across the room. For a moment you cling to the edge of the door with the feeling that everything is passing you too fast and you cannot catch up. Then through the corridors, running, through the saloon, the passages, onto the lower catwalk. Walking quickly now, grasping the handrail.

The blaze of the sinking missile carrier illuminates the sleek shapes of the big French Mirage 111-0's diving in with an entourage of Swedish SAAB fighters, cannons flickering. Chewing up great wide furrows of pulpy froth across the sea lily.

The Lily. *It's dying.*

Down the fifty feet of ladder to where the leaves are decaying swiftly, into a putrescent jelly. Nauseating smell makes your stomach buck. Two of the three seed pods are crackling popping bonfires. Coughing and retching you start out towards the undamaged one. Struggle through a knee-deep bog of stinking gluey fronds. Freezing cold tears, bites into your legs. Rain lashing into your face, partially blinding you and soaking through your clothes. Fighters yell past lacing the night with burning streamers of white which explodes into an already crippled destroyer. Jump across this trench of green pus and *splash* deep into sea water. Thrashing around wildly, spitting, sneezing, climb to safety on the firm swell of the seed pod. Gulping brine, mouth open, fluid pouring from your nostrils. Find something sharp to open the pod. Your numbed fingers claw into the jacket pockets to withdraw a sodden lump of grey linen handkerchief, one eraser, one cufflink, and a threepenny bit. To the south fighters are bunching for another attack. Climb higher up the wet slippery mound. A knife, must find a knife. Your hand rips half of your trouser pocket away as you withdraw a long thin object. A ball point pen. The jets are rushing towards you, hugging close to the sea. Leaning on your elbow you plunge the pen into the taut stretched skin and rend it apart. Gush of lemonish liquid spraying seeds like tiny starfish over your face. And you laugh. Deafening whoop as the fighters pass above.

Shells punch into the pod and it erupts kicking you back into the gooey trench, and unconsciousness.

It's cold.

It's January.

It's Friday the thirteenth.

And you've got creeping pneumonia. But better here among the snow-blanched hills behind Campbeltown than in an English prison subjected to their mockery, ridicule, and sick scorn.

It is almost a month since you first felt their hate, anybody's hate, very painfully upon waking up in that trench with a group of roustabouts wading in at your ribs with their heavy boots. They would probably have killed you had not Beattie stopped them, and he in his turn would probably have killed you had not the sailors arrived to place you under arrest. Then you were dragged through a crowd of howling angry men.

Prescott pushed his way to the front screaming 'Slime sucking pig's bastard of a murderer. She was going to be my fiancée and you ruined her. Ruined her,' and spat a greaser right into your face. He ranted on until someone pulled the babbling fool aside.

You did not see Sir Martin Amherst but that is perhaps quite fortunate considering that he is now in an institution for the criminally insane. After the Lily's death he was summoned to appear before the Minister to explain his negligence and distortion of facts and deliberate tampering with specimens and why he did not take action when the situation got 'out of hand'. The Minister had been putting the needle on Amherst for almost a year, so when the knight arrived he brought a meat cleaver in his brief case. But then quite a number of people reacted violently to recovery from Lilylove, others just had ordinary breakdowns. A total of over five millions for the mental hospitals.

— More nuts
  Than in
  Brazil.

The navy boys put you in a launch and then you were sailing away from the rig with voices crying to you, downwind from the rig.

'You'll pay for it. Just wait.'

'We'll get you, Jalovec.'

'Rot in Hell and damnation scumrat.'

Polarity is once again reversed. But whereas you were merely despised before the Lily you are now loathed vehemently. Equal and opposite reactions.

From disdain, to love, to hatred.

You were landed at Grangemouth and handed over to the joyous arms of the police. Glad that trade was at last picking up.

There was no point in putting you in prison. They were all empty and staffless so you were driven straight through the early morning to Glasgow.

There to await transfer to London for trial and eventual imprisonment if not execution.

And it was in the Police Headquarters at St Andrew's Square, sitting in front of a single bar electric fire with a tall blond sergeant and two constables, that the news came over the small radio set beside the telephone.

'...*Legal history was made today when Dr Fenella Daily, one of the scientists at work on the sea lily during the crisis, was granted permission to have an operation for abortion carried out upon her. The father of the unborn child is known to be ...*'

That was the heartbreaker.

There was a sudden hardening of the spiritual arteries. Came bitterness. And a warm healthy hatred all of your very own.

At quarter to two the soldiers arrived. Seven men, big slabs of granite for their chests, muscles galore, to escort you to the station and thence to England. Strangely enough there was no crowd awaiting you, crying for blood. Probably your presence had been kept secret from the citizens of this flourishing city to prevent any outbreaks of rioting during your four weeks stay in their midst. A wise decision. Only eleven days ago the annual Celtic-Rangers football feud to celebrate the New Year ended in a full-scale religious battle. Butchery. Carnage. Reaction to Lilylove.

    — Celtic green and Rangers blue.
      They painted
      The town
      Red.

You were taken in a covered jeep to the Central Station and told that you would be waiting in the vehicle for a half hour until it was time for the train to leave. Then you would be taken on board. After ten minutes the soldiers were becoming slightly restless. The captain in charge of them seemed to regard this as a symptom of nicotine starvation and sent two of his men out for

cigarettes and a couple of bottles of export before the pubs closed.
— That left five.

Almost dreamily you bent down, picked up the machine pistol which one of them had left and fired a couple of short bursts.
— That left none.

Dazed you sat staring in disbelief at the slumped figures expecting them to jump up and pull the weapon away from your grasp. But they didn't. They just lay there, eyes open, with holes in their faces. Dropping the gun you vaulted out of the back of the jeep and sprinted down Gordon Street.

There is a remarkably straightforward method of getting your hands on some ready small change if you are financially defunct. You approach a shop front with a 'pennies for the blind' figure in the doorway. This is usually a 'blind boy' or a 'Sooty'. When passers-by see you struggling along the street with one of these they at first frown, and then realising that Students' Charities Day is only about a fortnight distant smile tolerantly. Two actually told you what a wonderful cause it was and dropped cash in the box. Having trailed four of these up side streets and battered them apart with a section of exhaust pipe yanked from a double-parked Mark X Jag you found yourself in pocket to the strength of twenty-three and sevenpence.

Quarter past three and a small red and cream bus draws out of Killermont Street bus station. You were the third seat from the end on the port side. And you overheard the little chubby conductor mentioning to one of the other passengers that it had seldom snowed in Campbeltown since the last war.

—Well by
    God it's
        Certainly making up for it tonight.

The night, screeching blizzard that it is, stretches on, and you search vainly for shelter. There is a distillery somewhere around; now if you could only find that — haha.

The hour after hour of cold becoming more and more intense. Crawling like arctic ants eating through skin flesh and bone into the marrow. Then agony. Sitting on the frigid hillside with the bubbling and racking sobs of a four year old, legs stretched out before you. Rasping her name and punching through the drifting white at the marble earth.

Off with the shoes, and the socks. Rub the feet. Slap those toes, again. When they are all red and healthy it's up. It's tramp trampy once more.

This you suppose is a singular suicide. But it is a suicide. The police will not be long about catching you. It's a wonder that they didn't before you left the city. Ideally you should drown yourself. But the water down there in the sea must be near freezing. So hunt among your pockets for anything suitable for wrist slashing. If only you could find the distillery. Go for a swim in the whisky. Beautiful death! Mmm. What is this in the breast pocket?

Approximately the size of your thumbnail, and like a small plastic starfish with three arms.

One seed.

The sky is hanging very pale, very ill up in the east. The fall turns raindrops which leave tiny punctures in the snow, turns rain which makes a steel coloured mess of the snow. Downpour. No snow.

Running over the fields, across the road, vault a dyke or two, beeline for the briny, your feet hitting the slush with the sounds of a messy eater slopping food. Right enough you're hungry though.

Across a pebble beach. To where the water licks against the rocks. stand there for a moment on the shore gazing greedily at the sweet seed. And then you throw it. Watch it *splash* into a wave. Look. It's fizzing away like an indigestion tablet; and there are a few seconds of the old questions; what is ...? from where ...? *Who gives a damn anyway?*

    — Each stood upon the sea lily
      New freed from love's cocoon
      And said he'd get you for it
      But they spoke
      Too bloody
      Soon.

It was Chris Boyce who first suggested the Glasgow Herald *SF short story competition, which I have organised for four years so far. With the range of entries we received it's unusual for the judges to be in full agreement, but in the first year Chris, Archie Roy, Alasdair Gray and I all placed* Mr Loom Projects *by David Lee in the top three. Like* The Rig *this is a story of love, slightly more conventional, but beautifully told within the competition limit of 2,000 words.*

David John Lee
MR LOOM PROJECTS

WHEN MR LOOM DROPPED WHAT LOOKED LIKE A marble into what looked like a small pinball machine, the inside of Beggarswold Civic Hall vanished in sunshine. From the direction of the east window a twenty-foot breaker heaved up its shoulders and rolled down on the audience, smothering them in spume, spreading and raking back the shingle on a beach that ran all the way from Beggarswold Highway to the Ickley Acid Yards no one had used since the shutdown of 'forty-two. Fabulous vegetation sprang from the sand where outside there were only disused lots, and miles of empty housing lay buried under cliffs taller and more monumental than anything to be seen on Earth.

'We had a barbecue here,' said Mr Loom.

He clicked out the little glass bead and once again they were closed up in semi-darkness. 'The next one ... '

He felt the show was going well, in spite of an early mishap when a dead moth caught in his old projector had appeared on Mrs d'Ariel's lap, blown up in three dimensions by a factor of two hundred and fifty. Dear Heaven, the screams! You'd have thought she was being dragged down live into Hades the way she carried on – not the sort of behaviour members of the Fond Memories Society, in their obligatory evening dress, would look on kindly.

' ... was taken the same day. I had to climb a bit, I don't mind telling you. There was some talk about moving those cliffs, but for some reason no one had got around to it.

Mr Loom said this in a way that suggested they all knew very well why no one had got around to it.

They were looking down from a slight elevation on to the same beach. From here the water was so transparent that pink shingle could be seen well out to sea; the sky they hadn't noticed in the previous scene now looked unusually lofty, with a scatter of hazy clouds: not the dull square ones induced on production planets, but full and promiscuous like a woman's hair. Clinging to the rocks you could detect a faint smell of — burnt cedar? lotus?

There were now two Mr Looms, the real one standing by his projector, and another version in white travel breeches seated with his arm around a dark-eyed girl.

'Hello!' said the younger Mr Loom.

'Hello, Geoffrey!' Mr Loom had planned this carefully. 'What's the weather like out there?'

'Very hot. Too hot for me really.'

'I'm sorry to hear that.'

'Who are these people?' asked the younger Mr Loom, gesturing vaguely out to sea.

'Just some friends, Geoffrey. And may I ask you – who's that pretty girl?'

'This one here? This is my daughter, Stephanie. Wave to the people, Stephanie – they're going to be my friends.'

'Hi!' said Stephanie, and duly waved at the ocean.

The couple sat together, grinning. Mrs Rhinegold, who was having to lean forward to keep her head out of the cliff, asked, 'And why did your daughter go to Paradiso?'

'She was sent,' said Mr Loom, 'with the Immigration Service.'

'Oh,' said Mrs Rhinegold, then, 'What were they doing out there?'

'They were running a promotion.'

'Oh yes, I remember. Harriet – what was it called?'

'*Down to Earth*,' said Mr Doon Binny.

It was the time when the word *scatosphere* first appeared in environmental handbooks; when travellers made jokes about black holes and putting your garbage in the planet provided. Somewhere deep in the bureaucracy of Earth government, nerves had twitched. Reports were written, committees formed. Civil servants slowly came round to the view that progress (which on Earth meant ruthless economic pragmatism) had left behind it a sort of excrement which became known in official circles as the Mess. Plans to clean the Mess up were put forward, but since nobody wanted to finance them it was decided almost unanimously to resort to a science Earth was known to excel in – the PR job.

'And a bloody waste of time it was too,' added Mr Doon Binny.

'You mean it didn't work?' said Mrs Rhinegold.

'I mean,' said Mr Doon Binny, 'it should never have happened in the first place. Going round the galaxy asking spagoes to came home. What an insult to — '

'George, you mustn't talk about them like that.'

'That's what they are, isn't it – spagoes? We shouldn't let them back here if they come on their knees. And they will. Just you wait. Give them a couple of generations and they'll be turning up cap in hand — '

'Hello!' said the younger Mr Loom.

There was a sudden disconcerted pause.

'Very hot. Too hot for me, really. Who are these — ' Mr Loom cleared his throat loudly.

With a click his double disappeared, the cliff tilted level, and they were buried up to their necks in cement outside a plain rectangular building that managed, without the aid of a sign, to make every passer-by think the words *COME DOWN TO EARTH* in Roman italic. These monsters in telepathic brick, a trademark of Earth's short-lived galactic imperialism, could be seen in vast numbers wherever colonies had taken root. Locals (alien life forms, known colloquially as *greenguys*) often looked at them and wondered how creatures who arived by a means as sublime as interstellar slipway could bring with them objects so utterly pedestrian. This, combined with mankind's fondness for representing 3D surfaces on bits of paper, had in the early days given rise to a belief that the Earth was square.

'The Campaign Centre,' said Mr Loom, ducking into the road as someone walked over him. 'Stephanie said this is the most perfect piece of mathematics on Paradiso. They held a week-long Earth Gala inside while I was there – all air-conditioned, of course. That window,' he pointed to a narrow groove in the glossy grey facade, 'is Stephanie's office.'

Fifteen disembodied heads gazed up like beetles reading a tombstone. Another click.

'These were Stephanie's contacts.'

'Who?'

'Attachees like Stephanie were briefed to make personal contacts in the community and persuade them to re-emigrate.'

For a moment the members of Beggarswold Fond Memories Society stared dumbly at the little group of Paradisians, at their dark smiling faces and smooth variegated skin. 'Bloody spagoes,' muttered Mr Doon Binny.

'They look as if they're going somewhere,' said Mrs d'Ariel.

'Yes, I think they were off to the conch beds that day.'

'That doesn't sound very comfortable.'

'They go down there to blow the conches. You can hear them for miles.' Mr Loom smiled the smile of one who is in the know, and after a short silence Mrs d'Ariel said in a hushed whisper, 'Good heavens!'

'But don't they ever …work, make a living?' asked Mrs Rhinegold.

'Oh, they say they do. You see this one here?' Mr Loom stepped forward to lay his finger in the nose of a young woman with a child. He had to reach up to do it. 'Stephanie said she was a soft-surface geomorphologist. Don't ask me when she does it.' This brought a sibilant laugh from Mr Doon Binny. 'If she was a geomorphologist she'd have made her pile and come back.'

'Perhaps she doesn't want to make a pile, George.'

'Then I feel sorry for her.'

'She's got her little boy. There's more to life than making money.'

'And there's more to life than lazing around on some bloody little lagoon of a planet and leaving the rest of us to do the work.'

'The next one was taken inside the Gala hall ... '

'Good. About time we saw something worthwhile.'

They saw a sea of chairs arranged in blocks around a giant in a black one-piece flannel evening suit who was talking rapidly about employment prospects, conditions of service, tax benefits and pensions. This image had been projected like Mr Loom's moth from a low dais where, if you looked hard enough, you could just see a five-foot bald immigration rating mumbling into his notes. Behind him hung a curtain of flexible telepathic strips; beyond those an immense arena where walk-in walk-out projections were clustered like whirligigs at a fair. The sight was, as Mrs d'Ariel commented, 'absolutely awe-inspiring.'

'Why isn't there anybody there?' asked Mr Doon Binny.

'I don't know,' said Mr Loom, his gaze fixed on the giant's integrated tiepin. 'They just didn't seem to show a lot of interest.'

'It's shameful. Bloody shameful.'

'It's what it's like on Paradiso.' Mr Loom changed the beads. 'I thought you might like to see this. I had to take the camera into a projection to take it so it may be slightly fuzzy ...'

It was as though the walls of the building had fallen away and left them in Beggarsworld, but not the Beggarsworld they knew. The real Beggarswold, the post-space village clawed together from the sprawling industrial hinterland of the port of Glasgow-cum-North-England, sat in the middle of a waste land under skies that seemed to crack and bleed at dawn and close up in a dusty fog as the day wore on. Suddenly the skies were blue, the horizons clear, the city's leftovers transformed into an expanse of rolling parkland filled with the calls of a thousand tropical birds. Everything you looked at in this earthly paradise had been made, by a crafty combination of technologies, to exude the same, strong, subliminal image. *Come down to earth,* it said.

'By God, it's beautiful,' said Mr Doon Binny, delving for his handkerchief. 'And you mean to say nobody came to see that? It's a bloody disgrace.'

'No, they didn't come,' said Mr Loom. 'I don't know why.'

He switched off the projector, and the perfect geometrical interior of Beggarswold Civic Hall crystallised around them. There was rain outside.

'Well,' said Mrs Rhinegold, jumping up, 'I'm sure we'd all like to thank Mr Loom for his interesting and thought-provoking show. I often think, Mr Loom, how lucky we are to have such a travelled man amongst us. I only feel it is a pity, since her campaign on Paradiso has finished, that your daughter wasn't able to be with us tonight ... '

They rose, pushed back chairs and pulled on overcoats, said their goodbyes. Mr Loom opened the projector's carrying-case, but instead of dismantling the machine, he sat down again and sorted through the round films until he found the one he had not shown. He fed it in.

The shallow dunes were warm and bright and painted with the shadows of the great conches storms had thrown up on this ridge before man came. Stephanie had taken him to the largest of them, the one called the Angels' Trumpet, and they had stood at the foot of the ladder Paradisians climbed to take their turn at blowing. The long, low, beautiful sounds of other conches came in on them like a gentle evening breeze. No one had been able to play this Angels' Trumpet; if one day they did, it was said, the sound would be heard on the other side of the galaxy and draw every living creature there.

Mr Loom watched for a minute as his daughter and his younger self stood side by side, shading their eyes from the sun. Then with ritual calm he moved deeper into the projection and, taking great care as though he were balancing on a narrow wall, merged with his own image. It gave him a queasy, prickly sensation to look out over the dunes and feel the same tiny treacherous thrill he had felt on their last day together. When his daughter turned to him he stared indulgently into those bright, attentive eyes and caught in his breath the light unmistakable fragrance of Paradisian perfume; but she reached up to stroke his cheek with insubstantial fingers and then, laughing as she laid hold on the airy ladder, climbed up and away.

In the limited space available here, I won't even attempt to summarise Naomi Mitchison's wide range of literary output. Her interest in SF and fantasy goes back a long way: for years Allen & Unwin quoted her review of Volume 1 of The Lord of the Rings *as 'super science fiction ... timeless ... will go on and on'. Her own SF novel,* Memoirs of a Spacewoman *(1962) had considerable impact when women writers of SF were rare. Her appearance here demonstrates that major Scottish writers don't regard science fiction as a ghetto but as an imaginative field which they can enter or draw upon at will.*

Naomi Mitchison
WHAT KIND OF LESSON?

I REALLY DON'T KNOW WHETHER THESE PARALLEL worlds exist in any sense which we would recognise, or whether they have been thought up for some fairly adequate reason which I personally find of little interest. But also it is not my speciality. Communication, yes – but not with something completely unknown. Whether or not these worlds are objectively real, we find ourselves in them and have to make the best of it. Probably you know what I mean. I speak for those who can understand. If you have had a parallel experience, I trust you can look back with equanimity now that it is in the past.

These humanoids then, who inhabited, though sparsely, the world in question, had one main peculiarity: this was the algae in their tissues which kept them going with sufficient photosynthetic energy so long as there was a reasonable amount of sunshine, which there usually was. They ate as well, using apparently normal our-world digestive processes, such fungi, lichens and even occasional ferns as could be found, as well as seaweeds. But these on the whole only gave an illusion of fullness and its pleasures. There was no absolute need to eat, and often they went for long periods without doing so. In order to give the maximum exposure for the algae, they had webs between their fingers as well as between their toes, which were longer and more easily separated than those of their human semi-duplicates. In the delicate tissues of these webs the blood circulated near the surface, and so it did in the beautiful retractable ear-fans which they unfolded from either side of their faces. These were their main areas for decoration, with fine designs in what appeared to be gold, although this was something which could not be precisely ascertained, as all individuals were extremely shy of allowing any close inspection, let alone touch where these very delicate organs were concerned. Even a glance of admiration was sometimes enough to get the owner into at least a half-retracted pose.

It appeared to be essential to allow this process of photosynthesis to take place for several hours every day, but in the mild, often completely cloudless conditions of their present planet this was usually possible. It soon became apparent that there were two groups of algae, one green and one brownish red, and that these distinguished two groups of owners who were otherwise much the same. They had a curious kind of aversion from one another, especially when it came to the ear-fans, which either group would retract if approached by the others.

The weather in this parallel world was exceptionally mild, but they had shelters for the occasional storm, luckily always short so that at the end they felt depleted but could recover rapidly as soon as the sun shone again. Often they simply slept through a storm as they normally did at night, only waking at sunrise. These shelters were made with some kind of easily worked metal, usually gold, and a covering of a fabric which was fashioned out of a type of seaweed with a very large spread which could be made to take colours and which was also used for such clothing as they had. It seemed to be durable although often semi-transparent; it could however be made into strips and woven into something rather solider. This weaving always took place outside in full sunlight, as did dyeing and indeed any other pseudo-industrial process. But nobody worked hard; sunshine was free.

The main furnishing was for decoration rather than practical use, though they did have fires and did a little cooking. A few enjoyed the luxury of cushions made from the seaweed material, or screens against the wind. All seemed to take pleasure in designing new patterns for the ear-flaps of their friends, or perhaps, mates. They obviously enjoyed making small things while they lay out in the sunshine, feeling the photosynthetic replenishing going through their bodies. We were given various of these artefacts, but as you know, transfer from one parallel world to another is never very satisfactory. I was sorry not to get good replication of some of the musical instruments, mostly made from shells and their own long hair. These, combined with very sophisticated part singing, made up a usual background to photosynthesis. But the fine points were beyond me and my colleagues.

Gradually we were able to make contact or at least appear to do so, since we were never completely certain of the external reality of this other world and its inhabitants, who appeared to lead a so unfamiliar life although on a mental and aesthetic level comparable with our own. Something in the nature of poetry was often being composed among quivering ear-fans which, although not very intelligible, probably compared with much in our own world, especially as it was all geared into the music. One cannot of course assume that either our or their mental level was particularly high; we can in fact be moderately certain that somewhere in the cosmos there are other levels far out of our reach. But as I have tried to make clear, after what appeared to be much discussion and experiment, especially by myself, we did make contact. By 'we' I mean the group of colleagues with whom I appeared to be working – but as you know, in parallel world conditions there may be curious gaps and omissions and sudden appearances.

What came through from the humanoids on the other side was mainly anxiety about us. They recognised us as fellow beings, but felt we were not only ugly but in danger, as we had neither webs nor ear-fans, nor was it clear to them whether we were greens or browns. They felt it was most extraordinary when I tried to persuade them that we existed without photosynthesis.

In fact they could not really believe this. Their own surrounding fauna, in fact their pets, all depended as they did on algal colonies. Their favourite domesticated animal was a marine mollusc not unlike our own giant clam which, as we all know, normally has a symbiotic relation with algae in its mantle. But our giant clams have never been taught, as these were, not to bite. It was terrifying at first to find our new friends rocking softly on a cushion of mollusc tissue, the sun rays penetrating the shallow water, their ear-fans spread and wavering in the mild current about the ferocious grooved shells of their pets, which eagerly snatched up small fishes or other marine life.

Our friends were able, of course, to manage quite well below the surface in shallow water, so long as it let through enough sun to keep their algae occupied in converting the carbon dioxide from their bloodstream and keeping the oxygen supply up. But naturally they could not manage in deep or sunless water any better than we could. However, their beaches all tended to run out over softly shelving pale sand. There was another sea beast, a kind of transparent crab, which I never could get quite to like, though I am able to admit that it smelled pleasant: so different from the carnivores that we in our world seem still to prefer as pets. This crab also had a fanlike area in which photosynthesis went on; clearly this mattered aesthetically and even morally in the eyes of all those with whom we were gradually making contact, discovering, for instance, their main pleasure and pain sources.

Sex, we found, was fairly pleasurable and took place in a humanoid fashion, but more publicly than is usual in most of this-world cultures even today. Giving birth was distinctly pleasurable, especially, it seemed, the actual moment of expulsion of the small entities, often to an entrancing musical accompaniment. Then there was the excitement of spreading the ear-fans and webs of the newborn and watching the first pulsing of the rivulets of lifegiving flow. Sometimes there was an inadequate algae population, or the fans and webs had not completely developed. If these did not grow quickly, then death came. This happened sufficiently often to keep the population in balance, and affection did not develop until symbiosis was completely established in those who had lately been born. Then it seemed to come with a rush, not only to the mother, but to all the group.

The main unpleasantness in their sunbathed life was cloudy weather, languor and depression. It was at these moments that the adults sometimes died. When this happened, others of the group towed the body further out into deep water. Possibly the giant clams tidied everything up.

To reach this amount of contact between ourselves and them had taken a long time. Or perhaps not. Perhaps it would be inaccurate to speak of time in this connection. Certainly we ourselves and any chronometers which we had, appeared to keep curiously diverse notations. This is apt to happen in parallel world exploration (or whatever it is). All one can say is that we appeared to be making contact and that I found myself able to formulate quite elaborate ideas when contacting my small group of red-brown algae adults and children. All wore minimal clothing, sometimes on one part of the body, sometimes another. It did not appear to have any sexual reference, but it was apparent that those with the largest ear-fans and finger-webs could afford to cover more of the other parts of their bodies in which anyhow the blood vessels lay deeper so that photosynthesis was not very active.

As I have indicated most, if not all, of the humanoid population of this world spent their time along the coastal edges where the sun, about the brightness of our own Mediterranean sun, usually shone. The interior mountains were jagged and bare with nothing but lichens, bright coloured and brittle, until rather further down one came on the occasional bluish or orange fungus or fern. Among them we found a few lizards, all equipped with the usual algae and a double crest along their backs which could be spread, as well as a kind of fan-eared, mouselike creature with the same kind of development, and various insects in parallel with our own, all adapted to lichen eating combined with photosynthesis. At first our inland exploration yielded nothing of any apparent new interest or significance.

Naturally we wondered whether the symbiotic relationship which characterised this world had always existed or as nearly as one can ever say 'always'. This question became more acute when some of my colleagues found the remains of what seemed to be a solid building in the interior between two mountain clefts. It appeared to have been made of polished stone, though this was now roughened and discoloured by centuries of weather, even the mild weather of this planet. I communicated with the group to which I had become attached and which were usually somewhat concerned about me and my lack of symbiotic equipment. This would come up in some form almost every time we met. Clearly they were surprised to see me apparently alive and well whenever I came near them.

It was the usual sunny day. All lay on a patch of sand, basking. When I was with them I brought a red striped towel which I believe they supposed, or at least affected to suppose, was a genuine anatomical attachment. I always kept it round my shoulders so that it might appear to be attached. Whether or no they really believed this, it was clearly sensible to accept it. I began saying that we had been in the mountains. They thought we had gone there to eat lichens. I had in fact brought some down as a present. They had been prepared by soaking and heating and the addition of various powders whose names I have been told but whose origins – probably marine – were still obscure. Done like this they were palatable, but only just.

I went on to mention the building and immediately an unease seized the group. They shifted and whispered. Music, which had been playing desultorily in the background, ceased. Three or four folded their ear-fans and moved either into the water or on to a further patch of sand. It was difficult to know what was worrying them, but I finally got the communication that this was something which should be forgotten, which never was – or ought to be so considered never to have been. Should I go on? Perhaps not.

Yet it was one of this group who approached me later, alone. In humanoid terms Ssessa – the nearest I can get to the name – was a youngish woman of the red-brown algae group. She was much esteemed sexually and had already had three children of whom one had survived and two were forgotten, since they had been born with inadequate fans and webs. She wanted to know more about the building. I communicated to her all I knew and then suddenly she began to ask about our parallel world. This was the first time any of them had deliberately asked questions, though we had given them many opportunities. Would Ssessa like to see pictures? She would. I thought of running the machine, but then decided that still 3D colour pictures would be less disturbing.

Those of sea and shore which I deliberately chose to show Ssessa at first were not really disturbing, but gradually I moved to others: not yet cities or industrial scenes, but fields and woodland, such as we ourselves admire. And suddenly Ssessa was convulsed with grief, anger, what? I tried to get through to her. At least she used a word I had never heard and saying it, glanced round, then clapped her hand over her mouth. 'Again,' she said – I translate of course, and perhaps not accurately. She looked at the pictures hungrily and muttered the word. She stared at a picture of trees, a mixed forest, pine and beech and a few cherries and birch and such along the edge. 'But are they always – green?' she asked.

'Mostly,' I said. It was no time to discuss flower colours.

'Green,' she said, 'like *them*.' There was some disgust in her voice and I knew she must be thinking of the others whose symbiotic relationship was with green algae. She went on: 'And these – things – are with you now, this day, in your world? Now?'

'But with you,' I said, feeling, oh so cautiously, my way, 'they were – when?'

'Long long ago,' she said, 'before we were people – as we are now, as you see.' Tides of feeling washed over her face and neck, her ear-fans flushed and faded. 'Tell,' she said. 'Tell what other things you find there' – and she pointed towards the hills.

'Perhaps nothing,' I said soothingly, 'nothing to hurt.'

But she gave me a strange look, more disturbed than anything I had yet seen in that world, and then hurried away back to the sea.

My colleagues and I decided on further exploration. And what we came on shook us, for it was clearly the remains of very ancient wood where lintels and beams long gone to powder had been embedded into the stonework and so survived. Hundreds of years, perhaps thousands in this mainly dry and sunny atmosphere. So what did it mean? What had happened? Why? There were other remains of stonework partly covered with blown earth; it was possible that we might also find artefacts, but some historical clue had to be established.

Ssessa was there, her fans unfolded. A male was trying to interest her, stroking her two webs rather indecently, or so others seemed to think, to judge by looks and nudges and musical queries – for that was how they sounded. Her webs widened, then contracted. These creamy fans, beaded through by the algal coffee colour, were certainly pretty. Those with the green inlay less so to my eyes, and clearly to those of the browns. They were also erotic centres and no doubt would have been an interesting anatomical field of study had there been any opportunity. Ssessa saw me and stood up suddenly, disappointing the male. She questioned: 'You saw?' I had a small piece of crumbled ancient wood which I held out to her. Was it possible she would recognise it? She looked from it to me, raised a finger to touch, but could not bring herself to. 'The picture' she said.

I thought I understood, took out the 3D colour picture of the forest. 'That was once one of these,' I said. One could not say exactly what kind of tree it had been, only that in parallel worlds correspondences are probable.

Ssessa shivered. Then she said, very low: 'It is said – I have heard – long long ago – ' and broke off. I waited. 'There were – all these – ' she pointed to the picture. 'But not green. No. Never green, only a beautiful blue brown.'

Why not after all? We are so used to earth and chlorophyll in our terran leaves that we have to think again of ungreen trees.

But colours of course are in fact secondary though they have so many emotional connotations on all worlds. 'Yes,' I said, 'and people?'

'There were some like us. Partly like us.' She spoke with difficulty. 'So I have heard. In the sad music. Even before the change. They were our parents. They could still live. Not well but enough. Their children did better. Becoming like us.'

'But the change – what was it?' This was the big question. 'Everything died. Those – those big things that spread, that seem to have fans. Those that I see in the pictures of your world. And it is said there were little ones, many colours. Their children. Do you have them?'

'Yes,' I said, 'flowers. Lilies of the field.' But that meant nothing. 'Corn.' I said, 'that we make our food from. Ssessa, we poor things have to eat, often.'

But Ssessa shook her head. It was beyond her to understand about the necessity for eating or, as yet, that these strange things could in any way be food. She spoke again, painfully. 'All died in a short time,' she said, 'How long, you ask how long? We are not told. A hundred years. A thousand. It was the same in the end. Yes, they too had been, it was said, something we lived on. We people. The food of animals also. Big. As big as the biggest fish. But with legs. Do you understand?'

'Yes,' I said. 'Yes, Ssessa, we have those animals still.'

'That must be strange,' she said.

'Like this,' I said, and showed her pictures with cows and horses, dogs and elephants. I did not explain that some of these were also eaten by the people of our world. That would have been too strange and probably horrible. For a time Ssessa said nothing. My mind went racing back to the change. It appeared that all phanerogams had just disappeared. Why? How? And then could it happen in the parallel world? Our world? 'How long did it take them to die?' I asked gently.

Ssessa did not answer at first. Then 'We have only been told that – it happened. They became fewer. Smaller. The colours went away. They did not come again. It is not easy for me to think about it!' and she used a word I had never heard before. Then suddenly her ear-fans quivered violently and she cried out 'No! No! It never happened! It was told to frighten us! Not true, not true!' and she turned and ran back to the others. I watched her go, the fans expanding and contracting. I did not try to follow, but hoped that the male would be there to console her.

There happened to be a couple of the green algae group – or was it nation? – close by. They looked after her and laughed, not very pleasantly, cocking forward their green ear-fans. How fortunate that the necessity for lying in the sun stopped anything like fighting among the humanoids of the parallel world! But quite clearly I now had a piece of history. But how? Why? Did the phanerogams cease to be able to reproduce? Why did the lichens survive, the mosses, fungi and seaweeds, even the ocassional ferns? And how had the remote ancestors who were first able to use even a little photosynthesis mutated? It was an extraordinary jump to have made. And yet the jump which our own giant clams have made is unexplained.

I listened to the dying out of the pleasant music which Ssessa's group had been making. What had she communicated to them? Would I be hated because of it? A harsh sound from the shell instruments seemed to show something worse than unease. Would Ssessa avoid me now? I waited for the questions to stop pounding at me, but I believed that they had reached a peak point. The curve must now in some way return. Both for myself and for them.

This was the cusp, the moment when Ssessa and I collided and parted. As we all know from our own experience of parallel worlds, the descent from the peak of almost any such experience tends to disintegrate facts; certain episodes usually stand out, appear to imprint themselves on our memories. Here, I appear to remember that at some point Ssessa must have communicated warnings against the greens, who, she affirmed, were angry with us and would try to get rid of us because, in her explanation, they thought we were trying to find out – something. But what? Her communication was here blurred by emotions and the music that those called up. We were all somewhat alarmed, but in fact nothing happened and a system of defence which we had set up with some trouble and time wastage proved completely pointless. Probably both the greens and the red-browns felt that our habit of questioning was so alien and unpleasant that they reacted against it. Their world, after all, functioned not through questioning, but by taking things as they came; curiosity is a very our-world affliction. Or of course the main point of take-off, if that is the mood in which we use it.

There was, however, one unpleasant experience. We found ourselves encircled by a group of red-browns who all appeared much concerned with us. A rather lengthy attempt at communication ended with a nasty realisation of what they intended. Their concern for us had resulted in a determination to help us by innoculating us with algae while at the same time equipping us with ear-fans and finger-webs – they had decided that our toes were so unsatisfactory as not to be worth consideration. To do this they would take flaps of our skin and stretch it onto beautifully designed and constructed golden frames. Our external ears, when gristle, fat and such other useless parts as could be found had been removed, would stretch quite remarkably they said. We would find there was most satisfactory elasticity, and of course for adequate ear-fans the thinner the tissue the better. Skin from two neighbouring fingers would be joined up and the movement of the fingers would in itself provide considerable traction.

When we expressed our unwillingness to have all this performed on us, they explained carefully that any temporary discomfort would be more than compensated for by the well-being we were about to feel. Something we had never imagined! Could not have. But now! Hands were on us, Ssessa's and others; many and gentle, but decisive, with music backgrounding action. A touch of the knife. But you will realise that this is part of the descent from the cusp, quickening as we came nearer to the pull of our own world, our own time. With this rapidity of descent the moment of escape is blurred, as landscape blurs and brightens and blurs again in an earthward drop through cloud layers.

So, what were we to make of it? Or, since the group we were in is now dispersed, what do I make of it? Was it all a lesson? If that is the implication, what is to be learnt? First of all, in that world there could have been more exploration, more contact with the other groups, the other colours, but if once our genuine, loving contact had disappeared, as it must have done with the physical threat, our differences could not be halted. We began to distance ourselves whether or not we intended to do so. Reality began to thin out. We could not, perhaps, have survived the knife if it had been entirely real in our dimension. But you will all be familiar with the process of extrication from another world. One finds oneself in parallel with one's own. In a way this is sad; one has been offered an experience. This has to be enjoyed if possible, and certainly endured. But, as in the experience I have related, it may push us too far. And in the end, always, always, we are left with the unpleasantness, the anxiety, of a lesson put before us by what or whom or why is not known. Nor is it helpful to question or discuss. It must, we suppose, be a lesson intended to lead us further, to teach us something of the utmost importance. But this lesson is in an unknown and unknowable script or speech, and so, whatever our willingness, we cannot learn from it.

*After Naomi Mitchison's story about communication, and in view
of her long commitment to women's rights, it's fitting to continue
with Janice Galloway's* A Continuing Experiment. *This story was
the winner in the second year of the* Glasgow Herald *competition;
it could be set on Earth, now, or on some other world in the future,
but its relevance here and now is unmistakable.*

Janice Galloway
A CONTINUING EXPERIMENT

I CAN SEE THEM ALL ALONG THE FACING WALL,
working. Filling in their screens with symbols, opening and
closing their mouths. There is still so much to do and time is short,
so they keep hard at it, processing, correcting; working me out.

Together like this, they all look the same. Not deliberately
of course, but the air is very thick here and my sight suffers. The
weaker I become, the harder it gets, so now I can hardly tell one
from another. They don't come close enough any more, seldom
look in the way they used to. Unless they think they are alone.

Then, sometimes, they take a notion; move nearer to look
in at me with half-closed eyes, thinking. Mostly about themselves: what I signify for them, what they imagine me to be. A game.
Oh yes, they can get soft, sentimental then, wondering in front
of the glass with me dumb on the other side; just the two of us
before they go back to their data and their charts. My silence is
a great comfort.

I find, however, I read more clearly all the time. Without
effort. Nothing else to do, I suppose; killing time between rounds
of pain. And nothing else to see. Just them, all along the facing
wall, hazily working and opening and closing their mouths. The
floor is very cold and I don't lie on it. Even the softer things,
pillows and blankets, all bruise sooner or later and I lose sleep.
Everything here is so heavy and hard to bear, and looking out at
them is the worst.

I knew they were different from the start of course. We
all did. Though we had always felt the similarities more

significant. Same basic type, same physiological appearance, more or less – and both from an oxygenated planet so we had a lot in common. Still, we hadn't intended mixing. It wasn't necessary. We had everything ready for the repairs; just wear and tear, a little time damage to the outer casing that wouldn't take long.

We had everything we needed but the space, a bit of room. And we didn't even try to poach. We made it clear, asking through the radio waves, radar soundings; repeated requests for tolerance. A visitor should always knock. They saw us, too: a lot of flurry on the screens showed plenty of reaction, though there was no direct answer. We took it for indifference eventually. A mistake.

We chose a wide, flat area to come in, leaving plenty of room for error; our naive allowance for the necessary gap between theory and reality – preparing. The landing was rougher then expected, the ground not as stable, grating and shifting under the pressure. Then a lingering limbo while we waited for the reaction. It didn't come. We knew they were there all right but they didn't surface, preferring a front of concealment while we felt them watching.

It kept up so long we began to wonder if we were breaching some etiquette in expecting them to come clean, admit they were watching. In the end it seemed best to us to accept the pretence and just go ahead as though we didn't know.

We thought it was what they wanted, even joked about it, tried to put ourselves in their place. Beside, we were tired of waiting and there were things that had been put off too long already. We made our final checks and embraced for luck. Then we went out.

Choking. Viscous fingers tunnelling into our lungs as we breathed. Taking in that thick atmosphere was unpleasant but not unbearable. Our eyes were streaming. For a while all we could do was get used to the weight. Ripples of heat gusted where they moved behind the rocks. They waited on while we tested our legs in the quagmire sand, finding our feet, content enough while we looked inept. It wasn't till we set to work, moving more easily and unpacking tools, that they acted. A sudden shiver set it off, then there was too much happening at once – all new to us and too much to follow clearly.

There was a lot of blurring, but we knew immediately something was badly wrong: a lot of fear was coming round the edges of the rock with them, glinting off the studs of their heavy suits, and we could feel the weapons, concealed and close to the skin.

This was their own territory, mapped by their custom. They were harder, heavier creatures, trained in intellect and sentiment like ourselves yet they were afraid of us. It was absurd. I laughed. But there was no answer, nothing above them but stiff silent air, thick as cloud over the dry rock. One of them flexed.

Pilot and navigator. We knew each other's reactions and needs without thought: complementary halves. Yet now, for the first time, we failed. My navigator was turning away and trying to run. It made no sense at the time but I have thought about it a great deal since. She was always sharper than I, more instinctive. Maybe she saw further. She ran while I stood still, trying to work on logic with that unfamiliar air worming in my throat. I stood looking on as they set about their work.

She had not gone far and the sand was already cloying, pulling her down. They could have taken her easily, slowly. But the suggestion of chase had started them surging, triggered that adrenalin they do so little to control, and they wanted pursuit. I know more now; how they foster it, let it pattern so much of what they do. Hunting. But here it showed wild. There was too much restraint when they overtook, three or four ar once, holding too hard.

I felt the wrench of her tearing away from me as the spirit shattered with the bones and I was alone with them. I turned back bloodless, and saw my own face reflected in the black points of their eyes. Then something terrible touched my skin.

I don't remember much of my first sight of the room, just whiteness and weight, and nothing is changed. It is still white and heavy and hard as rock. The trust exercises, dishes of food, the games and toys came in no particular order and are irrelevant. Behind everything is the pain. It marks the beginning and the end of this place, though there was also a comforting episode of confusion.

At first, you see, I had trouble working out what it was they were trying to do. I had taken it for granted that the thing that mattered was communication. It was important to me to reach, reassure: share our commonality so they would let me be and I could go back. But that was not their priority.

Yes, it was very difficult for me to grasp that at first. They would come and open and close their mouths at me or take readings of my breathing, my functioning; taking soundings from machines. I thought they were trying to reach. All the time I sent them their answers, my sensations; striving to get through. But they could not seem to feel.

More than that, they were fighting – when glimpses of me, freak insights started to penetrate, they blocked them out so meticulously it gave them headaches. Yet I went on because I did not understand, not for a long time. Hopelessness does not come easily. There was a lot of pain, a lot of desperate, wasted effort till slowly, slowly, I realised it was not me they were trying to find. Of course not.

There I was under their noses while they were looking for something else – something I was not, that they none the less wanted. And when they could not, they concluded it was not their search that was at fault but I.

I could not communicate. Their system, their very language was designed to block out everything but themselves and left no room for other ways. That was it.

Opening and closing their mouths was easier than reaching and they had been doing it so long now they thought it was the only way. I knew they would never reach me because they would not feel. Lack of practice.

That was when the real decline began. I refused their food and they came with needles, punishing me with a constant scream of raw matter into the vein, killing with kindness. Then more readings, more data. Strapped with wires, I took to watching them more. And I found I was reading more clearly.

They were growing tired and disappointed: they had wanted so much for me to be happier, regretted I would not try harder to give them what they wanted. They were sad I could not understand.

Then these headaches: they were getting in the way of concentration, holding things up. So they took pills. I was getting in the way of the hurting so they took a lot of pills. It kept their heads clear for the job.

It wasn't long before their disappointment led to the next stage. I was not sufficiently the same for them to be put off much longer, for a little pain to hold things up. Yet they were a little unhappy when their machines registered how much suffering they caused. It did not occur to them to stop.

Instead, they wondered if the readings were wrong, why, if they were not, I didn't struggle more, as though they didn't know it would be pointless for me to struggle. And undignified. It is so hard for them to admit they act from choice, and that I do too.

To see my passivity is not lack of insight, not failure. It is acceptance. But I am not the same species, not the same sex, and it is hard for them to see further than that. A new pain threshold made a neater solution for their moral dilemma and stopped the headaches too.

Besides, too much sentimentality gets in the way of the work and that is what they find significant. It is not even a religion, then, not even a moral. I am dying for their obsession. Their hunting.

Disappointment and the need for speed has made them sloppy. Indignities of handling, rare at first, are now routine. Telling themselves they do not mean to hurt, they go ahead, pushing those heavy, fisted hands about my body, over the skin and on, inside. I accept that now too, though, after the first violation, I lay for hours, bruising on the floor.

They were distressed, all right, but not deterred. Still so

much to do and I was getting weaker all the time, running out on them. So they go on; increase the experiments then analyse, working all along the facing wall while I worsen behind the glass.

But they do what they can. Keep me going. It matters for research, but they cannot put it off much longer. One day soon, the slow, impure air will begin congealing in the throat and they will have to make the last move. If I die from sickness, there may be an abnormality, something unidentifiable and wrong in their post-mortem and they do not want that to happen.

One day soon, then, they will have to come and make sure. They will come in as they always have. It is their door after all, not mine. They will look unhappy but determined. They do not want to be terrifying and they are hoping I relax: if I relax it will cause less pain, less anxiety all round.

These men. They want me to understand. They will share a look, the needle hidden clumsily behind one square hand as they come, and there will be terrible sadness in their eyes. They do not want to do it. But I am not the same species, not the same sex. They will keep on coming anyway.

After each Glasgow Herald *competition I've given a course in 'Science Fiction and Writing' at the Glasgow University Department of Adult and Continuing Education, and the first year's class decided to restart the Glasgow Science Fiction Circle, of which Chris Boyce and I had been members in its previous run in the early 70s. One of the members of that first year's class was Louise Turner, and since the entries are judged anonymously, it was a great pleasure to discover two years later that she was the 1988 winner.*

One of the favourite devices of SF writing is 'If this goes on . . .': taking some current trend and extrapolating it, satirically or in warning. Busman's Holiday *was written when Glasgow's bus services had just been deregulated, and unrestrained competition was producing chaos in the city. A century later, Louise Turner's character believes that she lives in the best of all possible worlds; but notice how many of her fellow Scots – willingly or unwillingly, and not for the first time in the nation's history – have found it necessary to leave.*

Louise Turner
BUSMAN'S HOLIDAY

HAVE YOU EVER HEARD ABOUT THE OLD DAYS, THE days when Glasgow was a city full of people? Most folks had cars then, and buses used to fill the streets. I only know because my Nan told me, and even she can't remember that far back. The sight of buses streaming up Renfield Street in the early morning sun must have been amazing, but now, as I wander Glasgow's deserted roads, I can hardly believe it.

My name's Rhona, and I'm seventeen. I'm going to be a bus-driver, and this year I'll be in my first bus-race. My Dad's a bus-driver – no, not *a* bus-driver, he's the best bus-driver in all Glasgow and, for the eighth year running, he's been picked to drive Lord Clydeside's bus in the race tomorrow. I live in a huge house in Pollokshields, with lots of grass and apple trees in the front garden. His Lordship believes that his busmen should get the best, and that's why he gave us the house.

Nan says that when she was a girl, she lived in a poxy little house in the east. That was before they all left, lured to the jobs in the south by rosy promises that drew them away. Our family hadn't the money to move away to where the jobs were two-a-penny, so we, like so many others, stayed. Now we don't speak to the English much, and they don't speak to us, hiding behind their wall down in the Borders. We look after ourselves okay here in Scotland, and we're doing just fine under the Bus Lords. They give us all we could need: food, work, education, medicine, everything. But it's people like us, the bus-drivers, who get the best; which isn't really surprising, as we support society itself, and I think we deserve it.

Everyone holds the busmen in respect; and, for one day every year, they get a chance to show their gratitude. That day is the day of the Bus Race, held traditionally on the afternoon of the Glasgow Fair. Everything depends on the race, because only the Bus Lord with the best driver can control Glasgow for one year.

Drivers like my Dad tell lots of stories about the old days, when the buses of Clydeside, Kelvin and Strathclyde all tried to outdo each other in the city, fighting against their rivals to provide a cheaper and better service for the community. Eventually, so they say, the Bus Lords offered us more as everyone left, keeping in touch with England when we no longer did so. As they grew more powerful and more influential, competition between them increased, and unrest occurred in the city, with the Bus Lords all trying to take direct control. Things got a wee bit out of hand, until the Bishop intervened, and, with infinite wisdom, decreed that a race between buses should take place, and whoever picked up most people in the shortest time would rule Glasgow. All that is history. Now we don't bother with the passengers (to tell you the truth, hardly anyone in Glasgow has even sat in a bus), but the race has remained the same, getting faster and more furious with every passing year. The entire city turns out to watch it, and the day has been declared a national holiday in honour of the busmen.

I hear the sound of hooves outside, and I run to the great glass door. Dad's back, leading our pony round to the grass behind the house. No one could ever wish for a better Dad than mine. He's tall and dark, and he wears a smart navy-blue uniform. He always looks proud, because he drives the Red-and-Yellow buses, and he knows they're the best. He knows he's the best, too. I run to meet him, and he turns to me, smiling.

'Well?' I ask.

'We'll win,' he says confidently. 'I was talking to Tom, mind, and he isnae driving for Lord Strathclyde this year. He's been training his Lordship's son, and the lad's bloody guid.'

'Not as good as you.'

'Och, Rhona. An old dog cannae keep its bone forever, you know. Maybe the Lord'll think it's time for someone else to lead us for a while.'

'Can I still come?'

'Aye, but you'd better not be sick. I'd never live it down!'

'I won't let you down, Dad.'

We go into the house, and sit down to dinner; beef from Renfrewshire, with carrots and tatties too, and elderberry wine from His Lordship's estate in Kilmacolm. It's worth a fortune, but Dad doesn't have to pay a thing, getting it all free in return for his services as a busman.

That night, before I go to bed, I pray and pray. I pray to God that we can win again, so the Lord of Clydeside can guide our city for another year. I can scarcely get to sleep, excitement at the knowledge that tomorrow will surely be the happiest day of my life making me toss and turn restlessly. At last, though, I feel myself drift away ...

... and then it is morning, and the sun blazes in through my window. I glance at the little clock on my bedside table, and it says five o'clock. I feel good, and somehow I know that we'll win. Sparrows are twittering on the roof outside as I get up and have a long relaxing bath, knowing that today I must look my very best. Then I get dressed, wearing my special clothes: a skirt of darkest navy with a lighter blouse, made of real cotton, and given to me by Lord Clydeside himself. I brush my hair, feeling every long strand spring to shining life. At last I am ready, and I go downstairs.

Dad is already in the kitchen, wearing his neatest uniform. He hands me a plate of bacon and egg, and we sit down to eat. I can scarcely eat a thing, and Nan fusses over me, scolding me for being so silly. Dad just laughs, and says he was exactly like that before his first race.

At six o' clock we leave for Paisley, our pony trotting briskly along overgrown roads, red-and-yellow cart gleaming. Dad urges her on, fire glowing in his grey eyes, the fire that only a natural busman knows. He's always been a talented driver, but he never raced until Mum died. She used to be an engineer, but she was killed in the crash of '63, and after that, Dad changed. He took to the racing, and now it's in his blood.

By eight o' clock we've reached Paisley, and turned our pony out in a field near the depot. I can see Dad's bus outside, engineers washing it down in preparation for the race, and topping up its fuel. Don't ask me where the fuel comes from. Nan thinks that Lord Clydeside owns a little oilfield down in the Clyde estuary, and that's how he can afford all the stuff from England, giving them oil in return. I'm sure Dad knows, but he won't say.

We pay a quick visit to the racing bus, which looms over me, as big as a house. Dad checks the engine, and then says to me, 'She looks fine to me, Rhona. Shall we go and see the old bus? It's nearly time to go, anyway.'

I feel a grin cross my face, and can hardly stop myself from breaking into a run. We hurry over to the huge shed, and there, standing in a shaft of sunlight which shines through a hole in the roof, is the old bus from London. Its engines are ticking over, filling the shed with a dim roar that makes the air quake around us. I gaze in wonder at it, staring at the vivid red-and-yellow paint, and reading the magic words, *Welcome aboard. We're going your way,* which are emblazoned along the side.

Dad ushers me into the back, and I make my way across the wooden floor, and sit at the very front, looking out over the bonnet at the activity going on outside. Dad climbs into the cab, and slips the engine into first gear. I've never been in a bus before, and here I am, sitting in the pride of the fleet. Dad turns the steering wheel, and the bus lumbers round with a thundering purr, like some ancient dragon waking in its den. We move slowly out into the sunshine, and then we're on our way; the other bus, ready for battle, following behind us. I want to sing, the controlled power of the bus beneath me making my spirit soar. And all the time the sun is beating down, turning the road ahead into a shimmering haze.

We drive through the ancient streets of Paisley, crowds gathering to watch as we pass, wishing us luck in the race ahead. We park outside Lord Clydeside's town house, the old Paisley town hall. Dad leaves his cab, and climbs up the steps to meet His Lordship. Lord Clydeside is already waiting just outside the vast doors, a bent and white-haired old man with a stick. He may be getting on now, but eyes still shine with wisdom, burning bright from his face and piercing the hearts of all who know him. He rules fairly and justly; and we, his people, love him.

He climbs slowly aboard the bus, and recognises my presence with a nod and a friendly smile. I feel myself blush with the honour of it; and Dad, returning to the cab, winks at me. Lord Clydeside climbs upstairs slowly, helped by his advisers. Then, when he is safe in his seat, his chief aide returns, and gives two sharp tugs to a cord which runs along the roof. A bell sounds loudly, ringing twice, and the bus starts off. We're on our way once more, heading for Glasgow, where the race will be at noon.

The streets of Glasgow are swarming with people, and street vendors are selling sweets, trinkets and flags in the colours of the three Bus Lords. It is a child's paradise, but I am a child no longer, and I don't belong with those ordinary people any more. We drive through the city, waving to our followers who lean out of rickety tenement buildings and crowd along the well-worn pavements, with red-and-yellow flags in their hands.

We draw up in George Square. Lord Kelvin Scottish is already there, and his bus is on the starting line. He is leaning against his car, the only car that still works in the whole of Scotland. It is blue, and it is very sleek and elegant, with the sculpture of a silver angel rearing at its bonnet. With him is his driver, an old hand like Dad, who knows the set route like the back of his hand. Lord Clydeside comes carefully down the narrow staircase, and joins Lord Kelvin Scottish with my father at his side. Our bus is manoeuvred over to a space beside the Kelvin one, and I go over to it, and take my place at the front along with the engineers and the other drivers.

I stare out of the window, and at last Lord Strathclyde arrives, in a black coach drawn by four magnificent black horses, orange ribbons braided in their manes and tails, and orange lines highlighting the glossy black panels. His bus comes too, painted boldly in the same colours. Lord Strathclyde steps out, and with him is his son: blond, not much older than me, and not bad looking. He might be good, but he'll never be as good as Dad.

I wait in excitement as the vows are taken. It's quite simple. There must be no bloodshed, no sabotage, and may the best driver win. The drivers shake hands, then go to their buses and start up the engines.

The Bishop holds up a large sign that says 'Stop', and then, when he is ready, quickly flips it to 'Go'. All three buses lurch away, reaching top gear before turning down Buchanan Street. This is where the leader will be established for the first stage.

I bite my lip, knowing that Kelvin have the advantage, as they're on the inside. But suddenly Dad is ahead, feigning a swerve to the left as they reach the opening. The Kelvin bus nearly hits a tree, and Dad has got through the narrow gap, hurtling past the sculpture of the flying bird, with the orange bus close behind him.

At the bottom of Buchanan Street he cuts the corner onto Argyle Street, nearly scraping the side of the bus against a building. He is well in the lead, but the orange bus is still there, and I hang on for dear life as we pass under the railway bridge.

The gap is closing; and Dad, determined to keep the lead, weaves from one side of the road to the other, the double-decker swaying dangerously as he does so. He's just ahead as we move through narrow side-streets, and then onto Sauchiehall Street, a road almost as wide as the river itself. The road cannot be blocked, so this is where buses can go as fast as the wind.

Dad jams his foot to the floor, and I can hear the engines at the rear grumbling loudly as we rattle along, the whole frame of the bus juddering in protest. We're neck and neck with the orange bus as we pass the museum, ivy clinging to a lichen-stained red building which is now as decayed as the gardens around it. I look up at the old tower of the university, standing like a sentinel amongst the ruin, and see that the Kelvin bus has made up for the ground that it lost. Then I cry out in disappoint-ment, for – turning into Byres Road – Lord Strathclyde's son barges his way in front of us, forcing us to take evasive action. He smiles at my father, his face confident, almost complacent.

He hugs the inside all the way up University Avenue, keeping in the lead. Dad's jaw is set, and his eyes are hard, but he cannot get ahead. At the bottom of the hill, though, the orange bus slows up for the corner. Our bus flies straight past him, almost overbalancing with the tight turn, but somehow righting itself and regaining the lead. It is reckless driving like that which marks a true busman, and the younger man hasn't quite found the courage yet. The Kelvin bus swings round the corner like a veteran, closing in on the orange bus.

Our position is assured now, and I feel giddy as we pass the tall buildings of Sauchiehall Street at top speed. Dad doesn't even slow up as we reach the precinct, the bus jolting across uneven paving stones and sending overhanging branches flying in all directions. Dad wrenches the steering-wheel round, and turns the corner at sixty miles an hour, sending the bus down Hope Street at a rate which sets my teeth on edge, and my hands are clamped tightly round the rail in front of me. I close my eyes as he takes the last two corners, barely braking as he does so.

It is only now, on the home straight, that I find the courage to look out once more. Dad is leaning forward in his seat, a manic grin on his face. The finishing tape is just ahead; and as we plough through it, Dad takes a hand from the wheel, shaking it in victory and defiance. He pulls up: and, by the time the other two finish, he is out talking to Lord Clydeside. For the sixth year running, we've won!

That evening, I sit at a long table in the City Chambers, feeling drowsy and dizzy with wine and happiness. Lord Strathclyde is making a speech, but I am hardly listening to him, as I have more important things on my mind. Lord Clydeside in his victory speech announced that my father is to be his successor as Bus Lord, which took Dad by just as much surprise as it took everyone else. And next year, I am to start my formal training as a bus driver, now I have finished school. Lord Clydeside told me that if I was half as good as Dad, I'd be a driver to be proud of. So now I am a real part of this world, and, as I look around me, I know I wouldn't swap it for anything.

'If this goes on ...' On 11th May 1989, the 'Sixth Column' of the Daily Telegraph *suggested that the British government's next target for privatisation should be the atmosphere. Angus Mc-Allister was well ahead of them. This story was a runner-up in the BBC's* Read All About It *competition, and Angus himself was a judge in the 1987 and 1988* Glasgow Herald *ones. When he isn't writing excellent fiction such as* The Krugg Syndrome *(Grafton, 1988), Angus lectures in law at Paisley College of Technology, and here gives us his expert opinion on that possible extension of the return to Victorian values.*

Angus McAllister
WHAT DREAMS MAY COME

THE FIRST LUNCH SHIFT WAS JUST BEGINNING AND the canteen was half empty. Lang carried his meal to the far end of the room, attended by his reflection in the wall length mirror, which lent the place spaciousness, making it seem like two parallel tunnels instead of one. More than one mirror was forbidden by law, to discourage agoraphobia.

Lang squeezed himself into the empty end booth. He waited for nearly ten minutes, nervously picking at his lunch, before Masterton arrived.

The other man insinuated himself into the seat opposite Lang and their knees collided under the narrow table. Lang leaned across to him. 'Have you got them?'

'Keep your voice down!' said Masterton. He adjusted position to improve his leg room and set his lunch out on the table. Lang tried to curb his impatience. Masterton looked furtively around, then brought a brown envelope from his briefcase. 'That'll be twenty units.'

'Twenty! But you said—'

'Sh!' said Masterton. 'They were harder to get than I thought. But these postcards are really something. Wonderful photography, the best views you're ever likely to see.'

Lang still hesitated.

'All right then, fifteen if you throw in an air cylinder. I'm running short this month.'

Lang remained unsure. He was running short too. Masterton re-opened his case and lifted the envelope. 'Stop,' said Lang. He brought out his wallet, handed Masterton three fives. Then he unclipped a cylinder from his belt and gave it to the other man. His hand trembled as he took the envelope in return.

He started to open it. 'For God's sake not here!' hissed Masterton. 'Do you want us both put on ice?' Lang closed the envelope. There was no pocket in his skin-tight tunic where it would not create an obvious bulge. He put the envelope in his briefcase.

A newcomer arrived and sat beside Lang. He was a large man, with the permanent stoop of one who never quite finds a high enough ceiling. Lang was crushed to the wall, his arms left barely free enough for eating. As soon as he had finished his meal, he left Masterton and returned to the office.

ALL AFTERNOON, he remained conscious of the envelope's presence, inches away from public view. He almost expected it to jump out of the case of its own accord, scattering the evidence of his depravity before the rest of the department. He wondered how they would react. Would they be as shocked as they seemed? Or would some of them try to sneak a look at the cards themselves, as they waited for the Air Police to pick him up?

On his way home, he stopped in the main hall of the office unit, to uplift a fresh cylinder from the Air Department booth. 'You're over-consuming this month,' said the official as he stamped Lang's air ration card. 'I hope your home credit's good, in case you need to overdraw.'

Lang joined the crowd of fellow workers who were making their way slowly to the exit, breathing as much as possible of the free office air before leaving their unit. In the airlock queue he met his friend Sanderson. 'How about that drink you've been promising me?' he asked Lang.

'Sorry Bob, not tonight.'

Sanderson smiled. 'Surely not Brenda again. Didn't you see her last night?'

'Yes.'

'This is really getting serious,' said Sanderson. 'How about tomorrow night? Or do you never miss a night?'

'I'll let you know,' said Lang. They put on their oxygen masks and went into the airlock. It was already full of people, crammed shoulder to shoulder to minimise air loss. The outer door opened as soon as the inner one shut. There was no need to equalise pressure; the only difference in the outside air was that it contained no oxygen.

He set off down the corridor, parting company from Sanderson. With no need for air conservation, the outer corridors were built more spaciously. Even the tallest men could walk without stooping. Even so, the human traffic was just as dense and his progress was slow until he joined the main conveyor. Then minutes later, he left it and took an elevator up the four levels to his home block.

As he approached his apartment, two red-tunicked members of the Air Police pushed quickly past. One of them carried an extra breathing kit. Lang wondered casually who their victim was.

In his mailbox, he found a small printed card with a blue border. It was from the Air Department. *It is noted that your air consumption is 500 units above the current quota. Please effect immediate economies. Failure to rectify within seven days will —*

Lang passed through the shoulder-hugging airlock into his cubicle. He sat down and re-read the card. How could he be so far in excess? He'd received such a card only once before, and that was after a series of private drinking parties with friends. But he couldn't remember any visitors at all in the past month, apart from Brenda.

He forgot the card as he brought Masterton's envelope from his briefcase. He started to open it, then the doorbell rang.

He quickly closed the envelope and, opening a drawer, hid it under one of his clean tunics. The doorbell rang again. He switched on the intercom. 'Who is it?'

'It's me,' said Brenda. 'What's keeping you?' Lang pulled the lever that released the outer lock. 'Come on in.'

A moment later, Brenda mushroomed from the airlock, enveloping him. The tiny room suddenly filled with woman. Her breasts, firmly outlined beneath her skin-tight tunic, pressed against his body as they kissed. Her discarded oxygen mask fell to the floor. He hugged her more closely, almost savouring the texture of her skin under the thin fabric.

'You're early,' he said.

'Complaining?'

He kissed her lightly on the nose. 'What does it look like?' They sat down on the cushioned floor. 'What do you want to do?' he asked her.

'What is there? Anything on TV?'

Lang pressed a switch and a screen lit up on the opposite wall. After trying a few channels, he settled for a crime drama. For a short while they watched the detective follow clues down narrow tunnels and crowded conveyors, saw him interview suspects in low ceilinged offices and cramped home units.

As usual, Brenda's presence in the confined space made it impossible for Lang to concentrate on anything else. They began to kiss again. He swung the bed down into position, covering nearly two thirds of the room's floor space, and began to unpeel her from her tunic. The TV drama played on unobserved.

AFTERWARDS they lay side by side on the bed, their breathing slowly returning to normal. Brenda reached out and increased the air intake. 'The air's foul in here.'

Lang turned it down again. 'I've got to economise.'

'For God's sake, David, I can hardly breathe.'

Lang increased it again, not as much as before. He turned up the cooler. 'I got a card from the Air Department today.'

'A blue or a red one?'

'A blue one.'

'Oh, that't all right then. It's the red ones you've got to worry about. And even then, it's ages before they do anything.'

'Have you had one?'

'Not a red one. But I've known people who have.'

'I still don't like it.'

'You worry too much.' She put her arm round him, pulled him closer. 'You don't think they *like* putting people on ice? It's just a last resort.'

They rested in silence for a time while the TV, temporarily, recaptured their attention.

AFTER BRENDA LEFT Lang went out for a walk, to help the unit's air and temperature return to normal. He hated going to sleep in an under-ventilated room, but didn't want to add to his over-consumption. The corridors were just as crowded as before; there was always some work shift coming on or off.

Back in bed, he retrieved the envelope from hiding and took out the postcards. They were old and dogeared and their colour was faded, but he hardly noticed. They were all photographs taken on the Earth's surface.

At first he couldn't make sense of them, having no experience of a perspective that was not limited by walls, ceilings or floors. But eventually he identified most of the landscape features, drawing upon his unofficial store of knowledge, gained from years of furtive gossip and speculation.

He saw the sea — could that *really* be water, the same stuff the Water Board meted out in stingy litres, in return for a growing slice of his salary? He saw mountains, acres of vegetation, magnificent, isolated houses. And he saw people.

People lying on beaches, walking down wide streets. People bathing in the sea, reflecting sunlight from their wet skin. People with yards of space between them, free from the heat and stench of one another's bodies. People whose diminutive appearance betrayed the true dimensions of their surroundings, giving some idea of the scale of the mountains and sea, of the amount of fresh, free air that extended around and above them into infinity.

He recalled tales about how vast volumes of air moved in great winds, how fresh water regularly rained in abundance from the sky. How people had to wrap themselves up against the elements, their energy resources needed for keeping warm instead of for dissipating the pent-up heat from large-scale underground living.

The photographs, he realised, must be centuries old, taken before the total land surface had been commandeered for food production, when there were still few enough people in existence for them all to live on the surface, breathing their fill of unrationed air.

Lang put the postcards away. He became conscious of the heat in the room, of the sweat covering his body, of the suffocating atmosphere. Going into the adjoining three-foot square compartment, which served as lavatory, kitchen and bathroom, he dampened a towel with a minute amount of water and wiped the sweat from his body.

He crouched on top of the bed and put his mouth to the air intake, just below the ceiling. Only the faintest draught brushed against his face. He turned up the air level, increasing the draught a little, then turned it back down, afraid of using too much. The cooler was at full power.

He lay down again. The walls and ceiling seemed nearer than before. He put out the light and tried to imagine them further back. Instead, they collapsed about him, pinning down his body, clutching at his throat. He put the light back on and lay on the bed, gasping. The room retreated to the size of a large coffin.

It was several hours before he was able to fall alseep.

A WEEK LATER he managed to fit in his drink with Sanderson. The bar they met in was relatively spacious. It was nearly twenty-five feet square and had four separate air inlets, one at each corner. A ceiling mirror gave the illusion of head room. On the bar counter, a single goldfish in a tiny tank added an exotic touch.

As usual, the place was crowded and they were lucky to

get a table. Sanderson bought two beers.

'You're not looking too good these days,' said his friend. 'That woman of yours must be wearing you out.'

'I haven't been sleeping too well.' Sanderson seemed about to say more, then stopped. 'David,' he said eventually, 'I know it's none of my business, but did Brenda tell you what happened to her last boyfriend?'

'Pete Emerson? He was put on ice for over-consumption. Still there, as far as I know. Why?'

'She never thought of sharing his sentence?'

'Why should he? It was his fault. Anyway, she was never really serious about him.'

'Brenda's a beautiful girl,' said Sanderson, with apparent irrelevance. He looked down at the table as he spoke. 'You know, it's not much fun getting put on ice. It's not just a matter of losing a chunk out of your life. Most people lose their jobs because of it.'

'I'm not quite sure what you're getting at,' said Lang,

The bar continued to fill up. All the tables were occupied. Between them, and at the counter, people stood, straitjacketed by one another's bodies, drinking what they could of the liquor and the air. Surrounding the table of the two friends, they gave Sanderson and Lang the apparent privacy of a human-walled booth.

Sanderson looked up and met Lang's eye. 'You've been seeing a lot of Brenda lately. Where do you meet? Her apartment or yours?'

'I wondered what this was leading up to,' said Lang angrily. He tried to stand up, but remained pinned to the table by the pressing crowd. 'You're calling her an air whore, is that it?' He violently straightened himself, displacing several people.

'I didn't say that,' Sanderson said.

'You did, as near as dammit.'

Sanderson grabbed his arm. 'Sit down, David.' Lang didn't move. 'Look David, I know how you feel about Brenda. Do you think I wanted to raise the subject?'

H

Lang sat down. 'All right,' he said, 'but you're wrong.'
'Very probably. Let's forget it.'

Presently, the barman called, 'Time up at table five.' Since most of the extortionate price of the drinks was for use of the air, there was a time limit on each round. 'Same again?' asked Lang. Sanderson nodded. Lang lifted the empty glasses and burrowed his way to the counter.

As he waited for the barman to refill the glasses, Lang noticed that the goldfish, previously listless, had begun to swim restlessly around. He watched it become steadily more frantic and make wild leaps to the surface. As the barman returned, it jumped right out of the tank and landed in front of Lang, fixing on him its round, despairing eyes, as if gasping to him for help. The barman put it back in the tank. 'Water needs changed,' he told Lang. 'Beats me why they bother to keep it if they grudge a little fresh water.' He filled a half-litre glass from the tank, replacing it with tap water. The goldfish settled down, relapsed into lethargy.

Lang paid for the drinks and took them away, the asphyxiated fish stare lodged in his memory.

Sanderson said, 'I see Henry Masterton got lifted.'

Lang tried to hide his surprise. 'When?'

'Yesterday. They caught him peddling illegal postcards. Pictures of the surface. Can't say I feel particularly sorry. I never did like the man.'

Lang made no reply. 'The trouble is,' said Sanderson, 'you still get people stupid enough to provide a market for that sort of thing. They think the law's repressive, making underground conditions even worse than they need be. What they don't realise it that it's only because we have no concept of larger spaces that we manage to keep sane at all.

'An air policeman once told me that nearly three quarters of those they put on ice are ex-surface workers, or customers of people like friend Masterton. Apparently it makes them use more air, makes over-consumption compulsive. It seems plausible. Who in his right mind would continue to over-consume after a red warning?'

'Who indeed.' Lang didn't mention that he'd received one that morning.

NEXT EVENING Lang asked Brenda to marry him. She seemed pleased, kissed him, but gave no immediate answer. 'Well, what do you say?' he asked.

'We've only known each other a month.'

'Do you love me?'

'David! What more must I do to prove it?'

'Marry me. We can get a family unit, nearly twice the size of this place. They say two can breathe as cheaply as one.'

'Like hell they can.'

'You mean you won't marry me?'

Brenda sighed. 'I mean I'll need time to think about it. What's the matter, David? You're terribly jumpy tonight.' She drew closer, ran her fingers through his hair. 'Aren't you happy the way we are?'

'Yes, but —'

She put her hand over his mouth, stopping further protests. He wanted to tell her about the red card, to arrange for future meetings in her apartment, but she wouldn't let him speak. She twisted her body round until she was half over him and began slowly to pull open his tunic. Her hand caressed the skin on his neck, his chest, his stomach — His will power drifted away. From below, she seemed to fill the tiny room, seemed to *be* the room. He was an embryo, enclosed in a breathing, sensual womb.

After she left, he watched TV for a while, then tried to sleep. He'd had to abandon his evening walk because his cylinder supply was too low.

The temperature was unbearably high, the air unbreathable. The room was shrinking again. He felt an overwhelming urge to run out of the door, escape from his prison. But there was nowhere to escape to. For an hour he lay, unable to sleep.

He thought of the postcards. Sanderson, he knew now, was right about them, but the desire to have a look, just for a moment, became obsessive. Despite a week's insomnia testifying to the contrary, he felt that seeing them would help him sleep, would set him free, in his imagination at least.

He hadn't meant to turn up the air supply, but found it unavoidable. A little extra made no detectable difference, so he turned the intake to full, just for a couple of minutes to get the room back to normal. He slowly went through the cards, concentrating on them, trying to project himself into their world. His breathing quickened as the fantasy took hold. He reached the last card and went back to the beginning.

He began to feel drowsy. Another minute, and he'd turn the air down. A minute went by. One more postcard, then he'd stop. He fell asleep.

He dreamt he lay on a wide beach, the sea lapping at his feet. Behind him, snow-capped mountains reached into the limitless sky. A cool wind blew in his face and he breathed deeply, filling his lungs.

Brenda appeared before him, her naked body wet and gleaming in the sun. She pulled him to his feet and, hand in hand, they ran along the beach. As they ran, their strides became longer, their footsteps lighter until they floated into the air. The mountains and sea fell away. There was nothing left but the pair of them, flying free through the endless, beautiful, intoxicating air.

Suddenly, his body became heavier and he began to lose height. Brenda's hand slipped from his and she was soon left far above him. He fell faster and faster and plunged into the sea. The water was warm, enveloping him, pouring into his mouth, stopping his breath. A persistent buzzing sounded in his ears.

He awoke as an oxygen mask was clamped on his face. The red-uniformed figure of an air policeman was bending over him. The emergency buzzer continued to sound and, beside the inlet for the discontinued air supply, a warning light flashed. Inserting a key in the control panel, the policeman switched both of them off.

He pulled Lang to his feet and gathered up the postcards, shaking his head as he pocketed them. 'Out you go,' he said, pushing

Lang towards the airlock.

Another policeman waited outside. He handcuffed himself to Lang and the three of them went down the corridor, providing a diversion for the inevitable crowd.

At the Air Department, an inspector interrogated him about the postcards. Then he sentenced him to three months' compulsory air restriction, the automatic penalty for ignoring a red warning. Was there anyone he wanted notified? Lang gave the names of his employers, Sanderson and Brenda. They asked him his relationship to Brenda. Would she be willing to share his sentence and cut the period in half? Lang said he didn't know. A policeman went off to phone Brenda. Before he returned, Lang had a premonition of the reply.

They took him to a long room whose walls were flanked, from floor to ceiling, with a series of shelves like open-sided coffins. Each contained a narrow bed, a drip-feed unit and an unconscious, shallow-breathing figure. Lang was given into the custody of an attendant in a white tunic who found him an empty shelf.

'Your first time?' asked the attendant, slipping a needle into Lang's arm. Lang nodded. 'There's nothing to it,' the attendant assured him. 'You go to sleep, you wake up, suddenly you're in credit again.'

Lang lost consciousness. His dream began again. The mountains, the sea, the sky, were all as before. Just as beautiful, just as unbelievable. But the wind was gone, the air warm, his body too heavy to move. When he tried to breathe, it seemed as if a steel band were clamped round his chest. He lay on the beach like a stranded fish, his mouth moving in a mute prayer to the tantalising heavens.

Edwin Morgan's international reputation as poet, writer and critic makes him another of the stars of our anthology. His poem sequence The Moons of Jupiter *was written just after the Voyager spacecraft flew past the planet in 1979, and was read at the 'High Jupiter' spaceflight exhibition which I helped to organise at Glasgow's Third Eye Centre that year.* The Particle Poems *are here by special request of Howard Firth, Director of the first Edinburgh Science Festival, after Prof. Morgan read them in the Science Fiction Poetry panel at the Book Fair.* The Dowser, *much more recent, is the first of three contributions here which all feature extensions of normal human senses.*

Edwin Morgan
THE PARTICLE POEMS

1

The old old old old particle
smiled. 'I grant you I'm not beautiful,'
he said, 'but I've got charm.
It's charm that's led me where I am.'

Opened up his bosom, showed me a quark.
It gleamed. He grinned like a clam. 'Sort
of heart, really, though I've got four.
They're in orbit, and what for

is a good question, unless to pump up
charm. I know I must look a frump
– just fishing – but seriously
would you not say I'm easily

the nearest thing to doom and centrehood
you've ever been unable to preclude?
Cathedrals – oh, antiquities and slime,
knucklebones, teeth five feet long, signs

and wonders, auks, knuckledusters,
twangs from armchairs, waters
waiting to break, cells waiting to squeak,
a sniff of freesia, a book

of hours, and hours themselves like days
in love, and even nanoseconds raised
by charm to higher powers, wait
until I make them, and fade.'

Shot off – never showed his age.

2.
The young particle screamed round the bend,
braked hard, broke.
His mother dozing in Manchuria
heard his last cry. A mare's ear twitched.
Dust, and dust, the wires sang.

3.
Three particles lived in mystical union.
They made knife, fork and spoon,
and earth, sea, and sky.
They made animal, vegetable, and mineral,
and faith, hope, and charity.
They made stop, caution, go
and hickory, dickory, dock.
They made yolk, white, and shell,
and hook, line, and sinker.
They made pounds, shillings, and pence,
and Goneril, Regan, and Cordelia.
They made Shadrach, Meshach, and Abednego,
and game, set, and match.

A wandering particle kidnapped one of them,
and the two that were left made day and night,
and lef,t and right, and right and wrong,
and black and white, and off and on,
but things werc nevcr quitc the same,
and two will always yearn for three.
They're after you, or me.

4.
Part particle and part idea, she
struggled through a throb of something.
A wheatear, or an ear of wheat?
How could she possibly know
beyond the shrill vibrations, sunny fibres, field?
What was the field but forces, surges?
To veins of green and veins of red
she was colour-blind. Well, she was blind.
But was she there at all –
when the wind ruffled that nest of growing things
and took its course in the sun?

5.
The particle that decided
got off its mark, but died.

6.
Their mausoleum
is a frozen silent flak.
The fractured tracks,
photographed, docket
dead dogfights,
bursts of no malice.
Almost pure direction
points its stream,
deflected, detected.

Better than ogam
or cuneiform the tracer
of telling particles
fans out angrily
itself, itself, itself –
who we were
were here, here,
we died at the crossroads
or we defected
or we raced ahead
to be burnt out.
Faint paths hardly score,
yet shake the lens, end
in lucider mosaics
of theory. Go,
bid the soldiers shoot.

THE MOONS OF JUPITER

1 Amalthea

I took a book with me to Amalthea
but never turned a page. It weighed like lead.
I squatted with it like a grey image
malleted into the rock, listlessly
reading, staring, rereading listlessly
sentences that never came to anything.
My very memory lay paralyzed
with everything else on that bent moon,
pulled down and dustbound, flattened, petrified
by gravitation, sweeping Jupiter's
more than half the sky with sentences
half-formed that never came to anything.
My tongue lay like a coil of iron, the planet
never heard a word. What did I say there?
My very memory is paralyzed.
The book has gone too – I know how it began
but that first sentence never came to anything.
'The local train, with its three coaches, pulled up
at Newleigh Station at half-past four … '
The tons of pages never moved, my knees
were tombs, and though slow Jupiter slid past,
my memory of it is paralyzed.
The stupid moon goes round. The local train,
with its three coaches pulled up at Newleigh Station
at half-past four, never comes to anything.
They rescued me with magnets, plucked me up
like dislocated yards of groaning mandrake.
The satellite engulfed the book in dust.

2 Io

The sulphur mines on Io were on strike
when we arrived. I can't say I'm surprised.
Seventy-five men had just been killed
in the fiercest eruption ever seen there.
I hardly recognised the grim volcano
with its rakish new crater and a leaning plume
two hundred miles high – like an ash tree,
someone said. Meanwhile the landscape burned,
not that it never burned before, but this
was roaring, sheeted, cruel. Empty
though not perfunctory funeral rites
had been performed; not a body was found.
The weird planetman's flute from friends in grief –
my god what a strange art it is, rising
so many million miles from home into
the raw thin cindery air – was the first sound
we heard when we stepped from the ship. We saw
the men huddled in knots, or walking slowly
with bent heads over the pumice beds, or still
and silent by the bank of the red lake.
The laser probes, the belts, the brilliant console
sat dark and motionless, crawled through by smoke.
Sulphur blew to choke the very soul.
We prospected beyond the lava-fields,
but the best sulphur's the most perilous.
The planetman must shoulder sorrow, great sacks
of pain, in places with no solace but
his own and what the winds and days may bring.

3 Europa

Boots and boats – in our bright orange gear
we were such an old-fashioned earthly lot
it seemed almost out of time-phase. We learned
or re-learned how to skate and ski, use snowshoes,
fish through ice-holes though not for fish. Soundings
and samples were our prey. We'd never grade
in years, far less in weeks, the infinite
play and glitter of watery Europa,
waters of crust ice, waters of deep ice,
waters of slush, of warm subcrustal springs,
waters of vapour, waters of water.
One day, and only one, we drilled right down
to something solid and so solid-hard
the drill-head screamed into the microphone
and broke, the film showed streaks of metal shards
whizzing across a band of basalt or
glimmery antediluvian turtle-shell
or cast-off titan miner's helmet or –
it must have been the metal scream that roused
our thought and fear and half desire we might
have had a living scream returned. Lightly
it sleeps, the imagination. On that smooth moon
men would be driven mad with many dreams,
hissing along the hill-less shining wastes,
or hearing the boat's engine chug the dark
apart, as if a curtain could be drawn
to let the living see even the dead
if they had once had life, if not that life.

4 Ganymede

Galileo would have been proud of Ganymede.
Who can call that marbled beauty dead?
Dark basins sweeping to a furrowed landfall,
gigantic bright-rayed craters, vestiges
and veils of ice and snow, black swirling grey,
grey veined with green, greens diffused in blues,
blue powdered into white: a king marble
rolled out, and set in place, from place to place.
We never landed, only photographed
and sent down probes from orbit; turbulence
on Jupiter was extreme, there was no lingering.
Is it beauty, or minerals, or knowledge
we take our expeditions for? What a question!
But is it What a question? Is it excitement,
or power, or understanding, or illumination
we take our expeditions for? Is it specimens,
or experiments, or spin-off, or fame, or evolution,
or necessity we take our expeditions for?
We are here, and our sons or our sons' sons
will be on Jupiter, and their sons' sons
at the star gate, leaving the fold of the sun.
I remember I drowsed off, dropped my notes,
with the image of Ganymede dancing before me.
They nudged me, smiling, said it was a judgement
for my wandering thoughts, what had got into me?
The satellite had iron and uranium.
We would be back. Well, that must be fine,
I teased them; had it gold, and asphodel?

5 Callisto

Scarred, cauterized, pocked and warty face:
you grin and gape and gawk and cock an ear
at us with craters, all blind, all deaf, all dumb,
toadback moon, brindled, brown and cold,
we plodded dryshod on your elephant-hide seas
and trundled gear from groove to groove, playing
the record of your past, imagining
the gross vales filled with unbombarded homes
they never had till we pitched nylon tents there:
radiation falling by the ton,
but days of meteorites long gone. Scatter
the yellow awnings, amaze the dust and ochre!
Frail and tough as flags we furnish out
the desolation. Even the greatest crater,
gouged as if a continent had struck it,
circled by rim on rim of ridges rippling
hundreds of miles over that slaty chaos,
cannot forbid our feet, our search, our songs.
I did not sing; the grave-like mounds and pits
reminded me of one grave long ago
on earth, when a high Lanarkshire wind
whipped out the tears men might be loath to show,
as if the autumn had a mercy I
could not give to myself, listening in shame
to the perfunctory priest and to my thoughts
that left us parted on a quarrel. These
memories, and love, go with the planetman
in duty and in hope from moon to moon.

THE DOWSER

With my forked branch of Lebanese cedar
I quarter the dunes like downs and guide
an invisible plough far over the sand.
But how to quarter such shifting acres
when the wind melts their shapes, and shadows
mass where all was bright before,
and landmarks walk like wraiths at noon?
All I know is that underneath,
how many miles no one can say,
an unbroken water table waits
like a lake; it has seen no bird or sail
in its long darkness, and no man;
not even pharaohs dug so far
for all their thirst, or thirst for glory,
or thrust-power of ten thousand slaves.
I tell you I can smell it though,
that water, I am old and black
and I know the manners of the sun
which makes me bend, not break. I lose
my ghostly footprints without complaint.
I put every mirage in its place
I watch the lizard make its lace.
Like one not quite blind I go
feeling for the sunken face.
So hot the days, the nights so cold,
I gather my white rags and sigh
but sighing step so steadily
that any vibrance in so deep
a lake would never fail to rise
towards the snowy cedar's bait.
Great desert, let your sweetness wake.

Elsie Donald's Dragonsniffer *was a runner-up in the first year of the* Glasgow Herald *competition, and the closest we have come yet to a fantasy winner. As Elsie shows us, even in a world of magic an ordinary sense can be of great value if properly trained and developed.*

Elsie Donald
DRAGONSNIFFER

DRAGONS SMELL METALLIC. OR MAYBE 'TIS MORE OF a taste. Have you ever taken a copper coin into your mouth? Even after it has gone your back teeth ache with the memory of it, and your stomach curdles. That is the nearest I can come to a dragon's smell. And the bigger the dragon, the stronger the smell.

I used to think that everyone could smell them, when I was young, on my father's farm. We kept a dragon in the yard there, just a little one, like a snake with four tiny legs and a crested head. A wonderful mouser it was, better than any cat, for it could follow the mice into their holes. It would hide in shadows and cracks during the day, out of the light, but I could find it by the smell, so my father always sent me to catch and show it to visitors.

One day the visitor was a dark-eyed man in dusty black. We had heard talk of a magician in the neighbourhood, so as soon as he drew up his cart and asked permission to water his horse, my father sent me to catch the dragon. It nipped my finger as I drew it out of its hole, but I caught it along the back between the two pairs of legs and ran back to my father. The visitor had got down from the cart and was speaking to him.

'Ah,' my father said as I ran up. 'See this, Master. There's not many farms around here can claim to use a dragon to clean out their vermin' – but I could see that the visitor was not impressed. He said, 'Not much of a dragon, that a child keeps as a plaything.' His voice was soft and strangely accented. Now I know it for the accent of breeding and learning, but in those days it merely sounded outlandish.

Annoyed enough to break silence before a stranger, I said,

'It's not tame, Master. I have to search for it every time, and it bit me, see,' holding out my finger. My father promptly cuffed me for insolence, but the visitor answered me seriously, 'How do you find a dragon that wishes to hide, and one so small at that?'

I glanced up at my father, who frowned, but the man had spoken to me directly and it would be greater discourtesy not to answer. 'By the smell, Master.'

He raised his eyebrows and looked at my father, who said, 'It is the boy's fancy, master. He says he can smell the beast. In truth, he always seems to know where it is, but ...' He spread his hands and shrugged.

'So,' said the stranger softly. Then, 'Do you know who I am?' We shook our heads.

'I am the Mage Horace.' He flung back his cloak. The clothing beneath was also black, but not so dusty. Somehow the gesture, together with the total confidence suddenly in his voice, transformed him in our eyes into someone lordly and worshipful.

'And I have it in mind to take an apprentice. You, boy, what is your name?'

'Gerald, Mas ... your Wor ... my Lord.'

'Well, Gerald, do you wish to be a farmer all your life?'

Now, I will not say that he laid a glamour on me, but of a sudden our yard seemed dark, and grey, and small, and he the only gateway to a world of colour and deeds.

Before I could answer, my father intervened. 'Now see here, Master – eh, good Master,' stumbling a bit as the Mage's eyes swung back to him, 'Begging your pardon, but don't go speaking to the boy like that, making him think he has a choice.'

'He has a choice,' said Horace. 'I have given it to him. To come with me and learn a skill and see other places – I do not promise more than that – or to stay here and learn another skill. Both honourable choices, but I think I know which one he will choose. Not all of us can smell dragons.'

It was the last sentence which decided me, of course, as he had meant it should. It swayed my father too, to hear that the Mage took my fancy seriously, yet did not disparage farming.

But there was the farm to think of, that cherished millstone that could reduce him and family to penury after a single bad season. He said firmly, 'You forget, Master, that he is not free to choose. He is my only son. I must have someone to work the farm after me.'

'You will have someone, Farmer. Your wife is with child, is she not?' It could have been a guess, it was the most common reason for the woman of the house not to greet a visitor, but again the serene confidence was impressive. My father nodded.

'And that child will love the farm and tend it gladly,' continued the Mage, 'while this one brings fame to it – and perhaps fortune. Turning to the matter of the fee … ' – my father brightened at the prospect of some material gain from my loss – 'I will waive it on this occasion. Come, come, Farmer,' noticing my father's glower, 'You are not selling the boy, you are apprenticing him to me. Normally I would charge you for that privilege. Be glad that I am generous.' And he turned away to see to his horse as though the matter were settled, which in fact it was. I had never had the chance to voice an opinion.

My mother wept a little when she heard the news, but she had always had dreams for me, dreams that could never have been fulfilled on our farm, so she dried her eyes and embraced me, then asked the Mage to stay for a meal, that she might have time to see to my clothes and food for the journey. In the end he stayed the night; and the next morning I bade my parents farewell, pointed out the dragon's hiding-place in the byre to the Mage once more, and then climbed on to the cart beside him and left my home. I was eight years old.

At first the Mage sought out opportunities to test my 'talent', as he called it. Our land has many dragons, though most are so small that they could hardly be told from the lizards, were it not that they prefer darkness to day. The Mage taught me that this is not from the evil of their natures, rather that unlike the lizards and snakes they do not need the sun to warm their blood, being warmed from within. Small dragons are tolerated, but let them grow above the height of a cat and the length of a lance and they begin to be a nuisance, ceasing to fear other beasts, and finally a menace, when man himself may become their prey. Then must a hero or a sorcerer do battle. But such monsters are rare indeed, dragons being exceedingly slow in growth.

It was in discovering dragons to my new Master that I learned that I could size the creatures by the strength of their smell - and that neither fruit, nor spice, nor anything else could disguise or overcome that smell. Of course my education did not end there. The Mage straightway taught me letters, and thereafter let me loose among the scrolls he carried in the cart. There must have been nearly a score of them, with half of which he disagreed, but he would let me form my own opinions before reasoning me out of them. Reason was my Master's delight, and learning his obsession.

He taught me to observe the countryside by day and the heavens by night, until I could foretell the weather, and find our way, and gather herbs for his many potions. He started to teach me the uses of some of these, though he freely admitted (to me, in private) that there many which were useless – 'No,' he would correct himself, 'Whose uses I have not yet divined.'

Above all he taught me to observe people. By the age of twelve I knew a man within five minutes of meeting him, perhaps better than he knew himself. Some we helped, some we used. I do not remember being proud or ashamed. I learned all the time, and was happy.

Then one day we came upon a village overrun with dragons – I smelled it from afar. With our approach the odour grew, until I was retching and ill, and imagining a dragon the size of a cathedral. The Mage grew apprehensive watching me; and would, I think, have turned back had not the villagers spotted us. Then his pride came to the fore, and he whipped up the horse a little to bring us in at a trot.

The villagers were pleased to see us, but hardly seemed in fear for their lives. The reason was soon made plain: of the scores of dragons infesting their home, none was above the length of a man's hand, some even smaller. They stole scraps and got underfoot, but they were desirous only of leaving. Cats and dogs grew fatter daily, for the dragons were too small to have any wits, and most of those which reached the countryside would fall to the predators there.

My Master was overjoyed. He had long held the opinion that dragons did not breed like ordinary beasts, but rather were fashioned from the hot, living rocks within the bowels of the earth – this internal heat enabling them to withstand the cold, and their place of birth explaining their preference for the dark. He had never before had the chance to put his theory to the test. Now he walked about the hill against which the village huddled, until he found a cave leading into its depths.

Observing several dragons issuing from the cave, he hurried back to our cart, where he found me eating an onion in a vain attempt to lessen the stench oppressing me. He had me bring torches and follow him to the cave. As he lit the first, he turned to me, saying: 'I will require that you accompany me, Gerald.' Then, already turning away, he added in a low voice: 'I cannot smell dragons.' I had known it for long enough, but his confession pleased me. I followed him into the hole.

As it turned out, he had little need of me. The passage led downwards, never branching nor turning. The gently-curving walls and roof might have been finished with metal tools, and my Master speculated that it was a forgotten mineshaft. The smell of dragon grew ever stronger, and as I walked behind Horace in the dark – for he carried the only lit torch – I idly pondered what could be used to mask it. Eventually I reasoned out an answer and asked my Master its validity. As he turned his head to answer me, the passage ended; and he stepped out into the nest-cavern. I caught a glimpse of the mother dragon, larger, than the greatest cathedral ever built; then her jaws came down upon the Mage, extinguishing the torch, and I turned and fled back up the way carved out of the rock by her passage. I fell heir to the cart and its contents, and was soon known as the Mage Gerald, in which profession I have continued since.

So now, Apprentice, you have heard my story. Know that if you remain with me you will learn, not spells and charms, but logic and reason, which same might have saved my late Master's life, had not the proof upon which he always insisted been so swift in appearing. For the conclusion I had reached was simple: the only thing which can hide the smell of a dragon is the smell of more dragons.

In our world electronic enhancement of the senses is already commonplace, and full integration of the human with the machine is hailed as the coming breakthrough in warfare. William King's story, which was a runner-up in the 1987 Glasgow Herald *competition, was written in reaction to the movie* Top Gun *and the American bombing of Libya: what will happen, he asks, when people with those role models can form full relationships with their machines – closer than relationships with people?*

William King
THE PRICE OF THEIR TOYS

NINE SECONDS TO IMPACT. CROSS CAN SEE THE Iranian desert rise to meet him, feel the surge of heat along his side. No, not his side, he reminds himself, his plane's side. The sleek side of his beloved F-51 Dragon. He is his plane, his plane is him. They are fused by biocircuitry and the terrible, terrible heat.

He scans the sky with radar eyes, searching for the man who has killed him, the plane that shot him down. He locates it, a hard pulse in his electronically amplified perception. Die, bastard he thinks, and flexes his claws. The missile is released, responding to his nerve impulses. It accelerates away from his falling body. He feels a click as it locks on to its target and it's away, no longer part of him. It ravens outwards, small and voracious, guided by its tiny, feral brain.

Cross looks back into his flight computer, trying to block out the pain. He replays the moves of the dogfight, wondering what he did wrong, how the Arab beat him. He blanks out the pain as he searches for the fatal error. He spots it. The Arab had released a cluster of missiles, hunter-killers; he thought he had lasered them but no. He had missed one. Damn. He has let the side down. Again.

Eight seconds to impact. Strange feedback is moving through the system. The intricate web of software that links his nervous system to the control systems of the Dragon is starting to unravel. He drifts in and out of his body. One second he is aware of the airflow around his sleek, powerful carbon-fibre shell, the next he feels his fingernails biting into the palms of his hands. For a moment he roars with the voice of his Rolls Royce engines, then he cries out in a man's voice, one he hardly recognises.

The missile is halfway to the Arab, hc feels it with his radar. The brown desert reels to his human eyes as the plane spins. He could eject, he thinks, but what's the point? Soon the whole Northern hemisphere may be smothered in a cloud of radioactive dust. He does not eject, but he knows the prospect of Armageddon is not his real reason.

Memory flashes, augmented by the processing power of the Dragon's computer, vividly real. Sandy and he stand outside their house overlooking the base airstrip. Sandy is shouting, tears streaming down her face. She is angry and baffled.

'You know your problem, John,' she snaps. 'You don't care about anything but your bloody planes. You don't care about me, about little Johnny. You've never cared.'

'That's not true,' he replies calmly. 'I love you. It's just that the training for these new man-airframe links takes so much time. It's my career, you've got to remember that.'

'Screw your career, John. I'm sick of this. Sick of you and your bloody jets. You're gonna have to make a choice. It's either me and your son or those bloody planes.'

He turns to look at her, then swivels his head to watch the Dragon taxiing along the runway, its long sleek form shimmering in the arc lights. When he looks back, Sandy is gone. He shrugs and watches the Dragon take off, entranced by its beauty.

Six seconds to impact. He tries to pull the plane's nose up, using the secondary systems and the joystick. No use, he does not have the muscle. The plane was designed to be unstable in flight, attitude corrected by banks of computers. The computers are not functioning. He cannot save the Dragon.

He remembers the briefing on the aircraft-carrier: the General's terse, matter-of-fact manner; the boyish, clean-shaven faces of his fellow-pilots; the faint, metallic tang of the below-decks air.

'This is the big one, boys. We're gonna show the Ayatollah not to screw with Uncle Sam. That's the last planeload of Americans his boys are going to blow up.'

Most of them smile except Malloy. Malloy can always be relied on to ask the wrong question.

'What about Ivan, sir? We're told that the Russian airforce is on standby. We're pretty close to their airspace.'

'Just a show of strength, a bluff. We're gonna call it. Ivan hasn't the balls to stand and fight. Remember Cuba.'

'What if they do, sir?'

The room is silent. Finally the General speaks. 'Blow the bastards away.'

Five seconds to impact. His missile has almost reached the MiG. Its pilot is pulling into a steep bank, trying to avoid it. It's a futile move, now that the missile has locked on. He watches the explosion. A clean kill. He feels proud: it's what he has been trained for.

For a second he is back in control of the plane, feels it like he feels his body, tries to pull up, but the flaps must have fused. Briefly he wonders whether the rest of the squadron have reached Tehran.

A wave of nausea passes through him. A flicker of images. His interview for the Naval Air Corps. A leather-faced old veteran smiles at him and asks, 'OK son, what makes you think Uncle Sam will put you in charge of 30 million dollars worth of aircraft?'

He smiles, feels his wet, sweat-slicked palms. 'For as long as I can remember, I've wanted to be a pilot,' he begins.

Sweaty bodies on the beach, Sandy's curves next to his. His uniform lies near her jeans in the sand. It's his first leave, back home from pilot school. He has flown jets. He is a man now.

Graduation. He salutes the base commander, then turns to walk from the rostrum. He manages a sober grin at his parents, his mother in her clean cotton dress, his father in the wheelchair that he has occupied since his motorcycle accident.

Four seconds to impact. Shocked, he realises what he has missed: the MiG. Not the old 31 of the Iranian airforce. It was a new one, the 63, the Vampire. Cluster missiles, Soviet pilot. The Russians have intervened. He realises that they have never been calling the Russians' bluff. It's the other way. The Russians are not going to be pushed around any more.

His father, impossibly large, is standing in front of him. He himself is crying, he is six years old. His father is wearing his old denim boiler-suit, smelling of oil and sweat. Gently he wipes the tears from the boy's face.

'Bobby Young hit me.'

'Well, hit him back.'

'He's bigger than me.'

'He's a bully. You can't let them push you around. If you do, they'll just keep doing it. Once you stand up to them, they run. They're all cowards at heart.'

'Did you ever stand up to one?'

'Sure.'

The next day he hits Bobby Young, who gives him the biggest beating of his life, but Bobby Young never picks on him again.

Three seconds to impact. He is crying. Tears run down his face. He sees the desert spin sickeningly, feels a tremor in the pit of his stomach. He can smell flesh burning. He can't feel it. Either he is in shock, or what's left of the plane's medical systems are pumping him full of anaesthetic. He cries because he wants to be one with his plane again, feel its immense strength carry him skywards.

He knows it will never happen. He blacks out.

Under a second to impact. The plane is disintegrating. He can feel it. He relishes the sensation, loving it even as it kills him. This is the sort of death that he knows. His life is measured in the oscillations of a quartz crystal heart. He is one with his plane again. It's all he has ever wanted.

Somewhere in the back of his mind it is morning. In the

clear summer light he runs through the long grass, a plastic model of a Phantom jet in his hand. He is bombing commies.

Nearby, his father crouches beside his Honda 750, a wrench in his hand, oil on his fingers. On the back porch his mother shakes her head knowingly.

'The only difference between men and boys,' she says, 'is the price of their toys.'

He stays with the plane. He pays the price. For a brief, ecstatic moment he burns cold-bright and clear, and then there is nothing except a burned-out shell and the endless, empty desert.

All three winners of the Glasgow Herald *competition have been controversial in one way or another. When David Crooks won the first one with a story set in the Tolbooth Bar and told in Glasgow dialect, we had self-appointed critics who felt this was too close to home. But an encounter with the alien in Glasgow can be just as cosmic in scope – and just as funny – as one in London, New York or San Francisco.*

David Crooks
SPACED OUT

SO ANYWAY AH'M JUST SITTIN THERE, HAVIN A WEE drink mindin ma own business, like, and this guy comes up an sits down beside me, an then he says, 'ye don't mind me sittin here? Nae body's seat, is it?'

'Aye, on ye go,' ah says. No skin off ma porridge, know whit ah mean.

So he starts talkin ti me. Ah don't know whit it is. Must be ma face or somethin. Ah always get the guy in the sheepskin coat that tells ye jokes aboot nuns and alsatians an that; or the spamheid wi his hair in his pint that starts tellin ye why Russia's no a socialist state.

So ah just sit there, waitin ti see whit this wan wis goany turn oot like. An he says ti me, 'ye don't mind me talking ti ye, Jim? Ah'm saying, ye dinny mind, eh?'

'Naw, sawright,' ah says. Honest, ah wis that bevvied ah didny care.

'Ye see,' he says, 'ah've got somethin ti tell ye. A wee confession, ye know.'

'Fire away,' ah says.

'Well,' he says, 'it's like this. You don't really know who ah am, dae ye?'

So ah looks at him, an ah can see that he isny Adolf Hitler or the Pope, so ah says, 'Naw!'

An he puts doon his pint, and he starts pokin holes in the air, an then he says, 'Ah mean, you just think ah'm an ordinary wee guy, don't ye? Well, ah'm no!'

'Well,' ah says, 'that's fine by me. OK pal?'

'Naw, don't get me wrong,' he says. 'No offence, Jim. Whit ah'm tryin ti say is, it's just that ah'm different.'

'Is that right?' ah says, thinkin he was goany tell me he wis a harry or somethin. Not that ah mind.

So anyway, he says, 'Aye. Actually, ah'm an alien, see?'

Now ah didny hear him right the first time, so ah got him ti say it again, an even then ah wisny very sure, so ah asked him if he wis foreign or somethin.

'Naw,' he says, 'I come fae Outer Space, ye know.'

Well ah thought he wis jokin. Ah mean, who wouldny? So ah says, 'Ah come fae the Drum. Same thing, intit?'

'Naw,' he says, 'ah'm serious.'

'Aw come on, pal,' ah says, 'pull the other wan, eh.'

'Ye don't believe me, dae ye?' he says. 'Ach well, dinny blame ye.' An then he starts sulkin inti his pint.

So ah takes a good look at him, an sure enough he's just a wee guy wi an old raincoat an baldy hair, an ah can see he likes the bevvy cause he's got a nose like a carrot stump. The pubs are full o' guys like him.

So anyway, ah thought ti masel, May as well have a bit o' a laugh here, eh boys? Ah mean, nothing better ti dae. So ah tellt him ah wis sorry, it was just that ah didny meet an alien every day, know whit ah mean. An he brightens up, an starts givin me aw this stuff aboot cosmic travel an that.

So ah just sat there deadpan, like, an he's goin on aboot how he's been here for two thousand years, and the place is OK, but he's gettin a bit pissed off, so he's goany shoot the craw, an this is him oot for a last wee drink afore he goes.

Ah mean, it was obvious that the guy's doo-lally, but well, it wis just a laugh, wintit? So ah starts windin him up, an askin him stuff, like whit he's dain here in the first place. An he says he works for this newspaper back in Barnyard Star or somethin like that, which is where he comes fae, and he got sent here wi bags o' tee-shirts an sunglasses, an folk are supposed ti come up ti him an say, *You are the man from the Barnyard Herald,* and he hands ower the merchandise.

'Is that a fact?' ah says. Ah mean, the guy had some imagination. 'So ye've been hangin roond here for two thousand years, jist waitin?'

'Aye,' he says, 'but naebody ever turned up. Still, a job's a job, intit? Fancy a pint?'

So he goes up ti the bar, an ah'm sittin watchin him, an honest, ye wouldny have thought it ti look at him. An when he gets back, he starts talkin ti me again, but ah canny even mind half o' it. Ah mean, ah'd been in the place since five o' clock. Ah wis miracked! For aw ah knew, it wisny even happenin.

So ah says ti him, 'Whit's it like bein a spaceman, then?'

An he says, 'Ach, it's OK, ah suppose.'

'Whit?' ah says. 'Like Star Wars an that?'

An he starts tellin me how aw they films are mince, an they make spaceships look like Ford Cortinas, nothin but lights an furry dice. 'It's no like that,' he says.

So ah gets him ti tell me aboot his ain spaceship, still havin a good laugh, like, ye know; an he starts comin oot wi aw this crap aboot environmental harmonisation or somethin. Ah mean, ah didny know whit song he wis singin, but he definitely knew aw the words.

'Aye,' he says, 'ah keep it jist along the road. Ye know Glasgow Cross?'

'Oh aye,' ah says. 'Ye mean the polis box?' thinkin that maybe he's been watchin Doctor Who.

'Naw,' he says. 'Ye know that big steeple?'

'Whit? Ye mean, right in the middle?'

'Aye,' he says, 'the Tolbooth. That's it.'

Now that wis definitely worth another pint. So when ah gets back fae the bar, ah says ti him, 'Right. On ye go. Prove it,' thinkin, well, that's him shattered.

'Wait a minute,' he says. 'You prove it isny!'

'But it's historical,' ah says. 'In books an that.'

'Ach,' he says, 'anybody can fake history. Dead easy.'

'But it's jist an auld buildin,' ah says. 'Ah even had a piss on it wan night.'

'So what does that prove, except it's waterproof? You ever been in it? Ye ever met anybody that's been in it? Well then!'

An he starts going on aboot how naebody can prove nothin, an there's no such things as facts, an ye've got ti stay septical, or else yer mind'll get poisoned wi Science.

'Aw come on,' ah says. 'Science is OK. Science made that pint o' heavy ye were just goany get me.'

'Science,' he says, 'is a big con.'

'Wait a minute,' ah says. 'It aw depends on yer point o' view.'

'That's it exactly,' he says, thumpin the table.' An that's how it's a con. Aw these guys with their point o' view tellin you that they're right. It's like you. You think that just because ah look like an ordinary wee guy that ah am jist an ordinary wee guy, but ah'm no. See whit ah mean? Ye canny go by appearances.'

Ah jist nodded, so he gies me a wee example.

'Right,' he says, 'there's you an Albert Einstein on a train at Glasgow Central, an the train starts movin oot the station at the speed o' light. Ye wi me?'

Ah wis, but ah wished ah wisny.

'So there's two things happens,' he says. 'First, if ye look at that big clock that hings fae the roof, the hands dinny move. Now, Albert says ti himself, "Ya beauty, ve have proved ze theory." But ah'm standing on the platform an ah can see the clock's stopped cause it's needin wound.'

'Is that a fact?' ah says.

'Naw,' he says, 'but the second thing is that cause yer travellin at the speed o' light, the driver thinks the signal at the end o' the platform's green instead o' red, an ye go crashin inti the eight fifteen fae Greenock Central. Wallop!'

So he sits back wi a big grin on his face, an he says, 'An the moral o' this story is: one, Science is garbage; an two, yer better goin by bus.'

'Mine's a pint o' heavy,' ah says.

So when he gets back wi the pints, ah says ti him, 'Two

thousand years? 's a long time, intit?'

'No really,' he says.

'Ye must of seen a few changes,' ah says, wonderin how long he can keep on makin it up.

'Aye,' he says, 'the place just isny the same. No like the old days.' An he starts hittin me wi aw this guff aboot St Mungo, an whit a nice man he wis, an how he helpt him oot wi a few miracles, and how he drew the plans for the Cathedral, an aw the folk he'd met.

'An then there wis Charles Rennie Mackintosh,' he says.

'Oh aye,' ah says. 'Him that invented they digestion pills?' But he jist ignored me.

'Nice guy, so he wis,' he says, 'but no aw that bright. Ah had a go at tellin him aboot four-dimensional architecture, and how it saves queuein for the bog in the mornin, but he couldny get the hang o' it. Tried it in the Art College, an made an arse o' it.'

'You should be on the telly,' ah says. 'Make a fortune.'

'Worst thing ah ever did,' he says.

'Whit wis that?'

'The telly,' he says.

Well, by this ah'd had enough. He wisny makin sense, an it wisny jist the bevvy. So ah says ti him, 'Well, it's been nice meetin ye, pal. See ye again sometime,' though ah wisny sure aboot the last bit. But when ah gets ti ma feet, the room starts movin.

'You OK, pal?' he says. 'C'moan ah'll gie ye a hand for a taxi'. An he grabs me, an asking me whit's the matter.

So ah tellt him. 'It's ma eyes,' ah says. 'Ah'm seein two o' everythin.'

'Well, ye know the reason for that, don't ye,' he says. 'There is two o' everythin. It's only when yer drunk enough that ye see the world as it really is, intit.'

Well, ah couldny argue wi that, could ah? So we gets outside, and the fresh air hits me, an ah'm wonderin whit the hell's goin on.

'Along ti the Cross,' he says. 'That's yer best chance.'

So there we go, doin the Glasgow Foxtrot doon Argyle Street, an he's tellin me how he's goany miss the old place: the bevvy on a Friday night; fish suppers; Hogmanay; Celtic Park on a Saturday.

'You a Tim?' ah says ti him.

'Naw,' he says, 'but ah'm a wee green man!' An he starts laughin. A right comedian, so he wis.

By this time we're just aboot at the Cross, an ah'm feelin a bit rough, an ah'm lookin for a Joe Baxi, but there wisny wan, an then he grabs ma airm, an he says,

'Listen!'

So ah listens, but aw ah can hear is some guy spewin his ring in a corner.

'D'ye hear it?' he says.

'Whit?'

'The music o' the spheres,' he says, an he just stands there lookin up inti the sky. So ah'm wonderin whit he's on aboot, so ah looks up, and there's aw these stars, millions o' them; like, just stars, ye know. But then they start gettin bigger and bigger, till they're like big bright toffee apples or somethin, an ah'm thinkin ti masel, Jeez-oh, must of been a bad pint.

An while aw this is goin on, ah starts hearin it, dead quiet at first, like a kinda singin in ma ears. But then it gets louder, an ah can hear it better, an it wis weird, like somebody takin an eppy on a piana, an ringin bells an playin wi a radio, aw at the wan time.

'That's no ma kinda music,' ah says, but he must of went away, cause he didny say nothin. An then there's this noise, like ah'm standin under the Niagara Falls, an the whole world starts meltin or somethin, an the buildins start movin like they're painted on water. Honest, ah wis pure dazzled, so ah wis. An then the next thing ah knew, ah wis lyin flat on ma back, an everythin's stopped movin, an it's quiet again. Ah mean, *really* quiet.

So ah just kinda lay there for a moment, thinkin ti masel, Well, that's the last time you get bevvied, pal. An then ah hears aw these sirens, an there's aw this commotion, ye know, an some guy's pickin me up, an askin me if ah'm OK.

'Ah'm fine,' ah says, an then ah sees it's a polis, so ah tellt ah'd just fell on the ice, an ah'd be on ma way.

'Haud on,' he says. 'Whit's the score here?' An he points ti this big hole in the road, right in the middle o' Glasgow Cross.

Well, ye could have slapped me wi a wet kipper.

'Ye'll never believe it,' ah says, an sure enough, he didny.

An so they brought us here, an gave us a cup o' tea, an then you came in an started askin me aw these questions, so ah've tellt ye the story, mister. Jist the way it happened. Honest, it's the truth, so it is. Well, at least ah think it is.

Oh, by the way, mister, there isny such a crime as Aidin and Abettin the Theft o' a Historic Buildin, sure there isny?

And now that you have the feel of the Glasgow patter … Glasgow is to be European City of Culture in 1990, and the announcement gave immediate rise to an irreverent magazine of comment, Culture City. *alburt plethora made his appearance as commentator and poet in the March 1988 issue, and without delay turned his attention to SF and the issues of extraterrestrial contact.*

alburt plethora
VENJINSS

see
ahparrintli
thurza rekordin
uv whael songz
on voijr three
thitl lasta trilian ieerz

beea fukn laff
iffit gits inturseptit
bih inturstellur aelian
whaelz
ih
thaell lissin tu thu songz
help help
weer beein torchurd and
kilt
bih theez wee byped basturts
pleez helpuss
wee arr sensitiv
intelijint
see goan mammalz
messij endz

thae big galactik whaelzl
bih lik that

atrosti
atrosti
weel fynd thu organizmz
risponsibl
an fuckn wyp thum owt
willuv huddit then
whin theez big hiooj
spaesships
thu syzuh thu moon apeer
thretnin iz fuk lyk
itl bih nae good saen
look
it wiz an axdint
wi didni meen it
ih
naw
aw theez spaess whaelz
flyin aboot in dethmobeelz
gawn
(inna pioor spaess axent
by thu wae)
kumander
look
therrz anuthr wannah
thae bypedz
whut
vaepuryz thu basturt

y well
yoo myt laff
but aw thu saem
it myt hapn ......

The very first entry received in the Glasgow Herald *competition raised the issue of communication and the use of language. Impressed as we all were by the evolved form of English Richard Hammersley had used, the concentration it requires prevented it from being printed in the weekend section of a newspaper. We all agreed that it had to be a runner-up. The story itself is an old one – as old as the institution of warfare but Richard uses it to make a chilling point about the future of electronic communication.*

Richard Hammersley
BIG FIVES

I HAVE NO IDEA how this correspondence was transmitted to my terminal, but I think that it speaks for itself.

LOONALAZ MAILOGRAMS INC

5.5.93

Terra blu n wite is

Loona gray

u prescence wod

lume today

Big Fives from Xia

```
***************
***************
***************
```
17.8.93

Grooved Marjine

Neety card ah! Weirze its handwize to write there but here no coms n eve rot wristmods this damp heet in. Side which ****************************** n we so laz direct not. 1 month already here bin. The trip just like ever was – groove then tubed,**beaut stars n what but final drag you viz? Lon more us ivans than trips past, there ***************************************n needed all. Camp usu, eats tin, crashes tin, roofs tin, quad lous, vee not. Jungle weirze is, more ter set the gross sun. Then lume purple as be 1 dim red sun 1 wee blu mune. Nighthouse San Dee Zoo sorta the dins cepting. Viz not etees fore, nor hear. R big grunts kinda *****************************dogs sorta blu but. Tinner headforms (if gen heady they). Xenobiologists n linguists coms no nuts goin. Corders also heet trashed. Us grode ivans snar down n void jus. If viz headform never over too soon. They the **** (as the spock them call) carbon-base carnivores be n ev*** *************************************n*********************** ************. ********************e skip.****************tools mayb*********************************cook pot.****************** ********************. If civilized be – who care? Live n jive kid, live n jive.

U mis n u man ev, to sack solo gain weirze is. This tour drawn not I hope, cos diire is. Ways, clear buzz-snakes outa trine go I got. Get **** detail. Gaff I busy not viz, write u just. Me luck write fas.

Double big fives
Xia

```
T            -                          X  W    -M  -
   B3465AX58921        S          IX (C          O  -
   2087)        U                        .
```

******UNVIEW HUMAN EYES BY******

1235 Aldrin Glide
Ciaotown, Brazil 8
Zap 156789492567023
13.11.93

Loved Xia

Jus u mail viz, a wile sure anyhow groove. Neety there sound, etees with n what. *Stinkpres* half it rub like ever. By no dum gobble form get done not. Vee for that leave. Break it / I beside you want, u need.

Mam cool be, at u months snags not. I e u miss think. Brand drapes top room for we buy, old trashed. U them viz must. Else drag n tinny n byte is cred so by. Dream you.

Big damp fives

Marjine

```
T                              M        M        -
W        Z    15678949256 7023          B     VII
         F      (C         0      2046)        .
```

******UNVIEW HUMAN EYES BY******

Stakeout Inc.

Zap 111777345777111

Finding for YOU

23.12.93

Dearest Marjine

Our sharing deepest. Our service n all human for, Xia Waker-Martinez (B3465AX58921) snuff. Effort best docdoing unworth of. As per contract said party with plasgold 200053.21 u cred dump.

All who tour Xia with groan do. As per contract, effects n remains rased been.

Real Big Fives A-1

Chaplaw (Copyright Orchard 2091)

pp Augustus Wetherby-Tze, FFSA, PhD
Field President

In all communications please quote ref NKV22/4892/1X

T   B   VII
F   (C   0   2046)   .

* * * * * ***UNVIEW HUMAN EYES BY*** * * * * *

Alasdair Gray's first novel, Lanark, *established him as one of the luminaries in the Scottish starfield. That novel and his collection* Unlikely Stories, Mostly *(Canongate, 1983) showed that he too crosses into SF or draws from it without any sense of a barrier.* Locus *said of his second novel* 1982: Janine *(Viking, 1984) that it extends science fiction into the wilderness of a man's mind, and that's a fair description of one strand – but only one strand – of a very complex narrative.*

Alasdair's stories tend to begin matter-of-factly and proceed with steady pace in quite unexpected directions. The Crank that Made the Revolution *and* The Cause of Some Recent Changes *both show the national respect for science and engineering which I mentioned earlier; respect, however, is not the same as reverence.*

Alasdair Gray
THE CRANK that MADE the REVOLUTION

NOWADAYS CESSNOCK IS A HEAVILY BUILT-UPON part of industrial Glasgow, but two hundred and seventy three years ago you would have seen something very different. You would have seen a swamp with a duck-pond in the middle and a few wretched hovels round the edge. The inmates of these hovels earned a living by knitting caps and mufflers for the inhabitants of Glasgow who, even then, wore almost nothing else. The money got from this back-breaking industry was pitifully inadequate. Old Cessnock was neither beautiful nor healthy. The only folk living there were too old or twisted by rheumatism to move out. Yet this dismal and uninteresting hamlet saw the beginning of that movement which historians call The Industrial Revolution; for here, in seventeen hundred and seven, was born Vague McMenamy, inventor of the crankshaft which made the Revolution possible.

There are no records to suggest that Vague McMenamy had parents. From his earliest days he seems to have lived with his Granny upon a diet of duck-eggs and the proceeds of the old lady's knitting. A German biographer has suggested that McMenamy's first name (Vague) was a nickname. The idea, of course, is laughable. No harder-headed, clearer-sighted individual than McMenamy ever existed, as his crankshaft proves. The learned Herr Professor is plainly ignorant of the fact that Vague is the Gaelic for Alexander. Yet it must be confessed that Vague was an introvert. While other boys were chasing the lassies or stoning each other he would stand for long hours on the edge of the duck-pond wondering how to improve his Granny's ducks.

Now, considered mechanically, a duck is not an efficient machine, for it has been designed to perform three wholly different and contradictory tasks, and consequently it does none of them outstandingly well. It flies, but not as expertly as the swallow, vulture or aeroplane. It swims, but not like a porpoise. It walks about, but not like you or me, for its legs are too short. Imagine a household appliance devised to shampoo carpets, mash potatoes and darn holes in socks whenever it feels like it. A duck is in a similar situation, and this made ducks offensive to McMenamy's dourly practical mind. He thought that since ducks spend most of their days in water they should be made to do it efficiently. With the aid of a friendly carpenter he made a boat-shaped container into which a duck was inserted. There was a hole at one end through which the head stuck out, allowing the animal to breathe, see and even eat; nonetheless it protested against the confinement by struggling to get out and in doing so its wings and legs drove the cranks which conveyed motion to a paddle-wheel on each side. On its maiden voyage the duck zig-zagged around the pond at a speed of thirty knots, which was three times faster than the maximum speed which the boats and ducks of the day had yet attained. McMenamy had converted a havering all-rounder into an efficient specialist. He was not yet thirteen years of age.

He did not stop there. If this crankshaft allowed one duck to drive a vessel three times faster than normal, how much faster would two, three or ten ducks drive it? McMenamy decided to carry the experiment as far as he could take it. He constructed a craft to be driven by every one of his Granny's seventeen ducks. It differed from the first vessel in other ways. The first had been a conventional boat shape propelled by paddles and constructed from wood. The second was cigar-shaped with a screw propeller at the rear, and McMenamy did not order it from the carpenter, but from the blacksmith. It was made of sheet iron. Without the seventeen heads and necks sticking up through the holes in the hull one would have mistaken it for a modern submarine. This is a fact worth pondering. A hundred years elapsed before *The Charlotte Dundas,* the world's first paddle streamer, clanked along the Forth and Clyde canal from Bowling. Fifty years after that the first ironclad screw-driven warship fired its first shot in the American Civil War. In two years the imagination of a humble cottage lad had covered ground which the world's foremost engineers took two generations to traverse in the following century. Vague was fifteen years old when he launched his second vessel. Quacking hysterically, it crossed the pond with such velocity that it struck the opposite bank at the moment of departure from the near one. Had it struck soil it would have embedded itself. Unluckily, it hit the roof of a tree, rebounded to the centre of the pond, overturned and sank. Every single duck was drowned.

In terms of human achievement, McMenamy's duckboat ranks with Leonardo Da Vinci's helicopter which was designed four hundred years before the engine which could have made it fly. Economically it was disastrous. Deprived of her ducks, McMenamy's Granny was compelled to knit faster than ever. She sat in her rocking-chair, knitting and rocking and rocking and knitting and McMenamy sat opposite, brooding upon what he could do to help. He noticed that the muscular energy his Granny used to handle the needles was no greater than the energy she used to rock the chair. His Granny, in fact was two sources of energy, one above the waist and one below, and only the upper source brought in money. If the power of her *legs* and *feet* could be channelled into the knitting she would work twice as fast, and his crankshaft made this possible. And so McMenamy built the

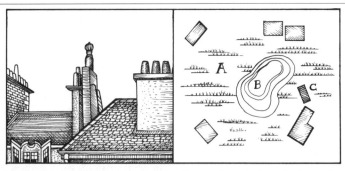

Left: Modern Cessnock shortly after the implementation of the smoke abatement act.
Right: Old Cessnock from General Roy's ordnance survey of 1739. Fig. A represents the swamp, B the duckpond, C the McMenamy hovel.

Left: Unimproved duck, after the watercolour by Peter Scott.
Right: McMenamy's Improved Duck.

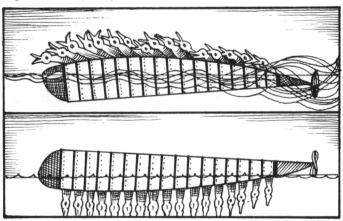

Above: McMenamy's Improved Duck Tandem .0005 seconds after launching.
Below: McMenamy's Improved Duck Tandem .05 seconds after launching. (The ducks, though not yet drowned, have been killed by the shock.)

world's first knitting frame, later nicknamed 'McMenamy's Knitting Granny'. Two needles, each a yard long, were slung from the kitchen ceiling so that the tips crossed at the correct angle. The motion was conveyed through crankshafts hinged to the rockers of a cast-iron rocking-chair mounted on rails below. McMenamy's Granny, furiously rocking it, had nothing to do with her hands but steer the woollen coils through the intricacies of purl and plain. When the McMenamys came to display their stock of caps and mufflers on the barrow in Glasgow's Barrowland that year, the strongest knitters in the West of Scotland, brawny big-muscled men of thirty and thirty-five, were astonished to see that old Mrs McMenamy had manufactured twice as much as they had.

Vague, however, was modest enough to know that his appliance was improvable. The power generated by a rocking-chair is limited, for it swings through a very flattened arc. His second knitting frame was powered by a see-saw. His Granny was installed on the end with the needles mounted in front of her. Hitherto, Vague had avoided operating his inventions himself, but now he courageously vaulted into the other end and set the mighty beam swinging up and down, up and down, with a velocity enabling his Granny to turn out no less than eight hundred and ninety caps and mufflers a week. At the next Glasgow Fair she brought to market as much produce as the other knitters put together, and was able to sell at half the normal price and still make a handsome profit. The other inhabitants of Cessnock were unable to sell their goods at all. With the desperation of starving men, they set fire to the McMenamy cottage and the machinery inside it. Vague and his Granny were forced to flee across the swamp, leaving their hard earned gold to melt among the flames. They fled to the Burgh of Paisley, and placed themselves under the protection of the Provost, and from that moment their troubles were at an end.

In 1727 Paisley was fortunate in having, as Provost, an unusually enlightened philanthropist, Sir Hector Coats. (No relation to the famous thread manufacturers of the following century.) He was moved by McMenamy's story and impressed by his dedication. He arranged for Vague to superintend the construction of a large knitting mill containing no less than twenty beam-balance knitting frames. Not only that, he employed Vague and his Granny to work one of them. For the next ten years Vague spent fourteen hours a day, six days a week, swinging up and down on the opposite end of the beam from the woman who had nourished and inspired him. It is unfortunate that he had no time to devote to scientific invention, but his only holidays were on a Sunday and Sir Hector was a good Christian who took stern measures against workmen who broke the Sabbath. At the age of thirty Vague McMenamy, overcome by vertigo, fell off the see-saw never to rise again. Strangely enough his Granny survived him by twenty-two years, toiling to the last at the machine which had been named after her. Her early days in the rocking-chair had no doubt prepared her for just such an end, but she must have been a remarkable old lady.

Thirty is not an advanced age and Vague's achievement was crowded into seven years between the ages of twelve and nineteen. In that time he invented the paddle boat and the ironclad, dealt a deathblow to the cottage knitting industry, and laid the foundations of the Scottish Textile Trade. When Arkwright, Cartwright, Wainright and Watt completed their own machines, McMenamy's crankshaft was in every one of them. Truly, he was the crank that made the Revolution possible.

McMenamy's tombstone, Paisley High Kirk, engraved for the 1861 edition of Samuel Smile's "Self Help". (This corner of the graveyard was flattened to make way for a new road in 1911.)

The CAUSE of SOME RECENT CHANGES

THE PAINTING DEPARTMENTS OF MODERN ART schools are full of discontented people. One day, Mildred said to me, 'I'm sick of wasting time. We start work at ten and tire after half an hour and the boys throw paper pellets at each other and the girls stand round the radiators talking. Then we get bored and go to the refectory and drink coffee and we aren't enjoying ourselves, but what else can we do? I'm tired of it. I want to do something vigorous and constructive!'

I said, 'Dig a tunnel.'

'What do you mean?'

'Instead of drinking coffee when you feel bored, go down to the basement and dig an escape tunnel.'

'But if I wanted to escape I could just walk through the front door and not come back.'

'You can't escape that way. The Corporation would stop your bursary and you would have to work for a living.'

'But where would I be escaping to?'

'That isn't important. To travel hopefully is better than to arrive.'

My suggestion was not meant seriously, but it gained much support in the painting department. In the seldom-visited sub-basement a flagstone was replaced by a disguised trap-door. Under this a room was dug into the school's foundation. The tunnel began here, and here the various shifts operated the winch which pulled up boxes of waste stuff, and put the waste into small sacks easily smuggled out under the clothing. The school was built on a bank of igneous quartz, so there was no danger of the walls caving in and no need of pit-props. Digging was simplified by the use of a chemical solvent which, applied to the rock surface with handspray, rendered it gravelly and workable. The credit for this invention belonged to the industrial design department. The students of this department despised the painters digging the tunnel but it interested them as a technical challenge. Without their help it could not have reached the depths it did.

In spite of the project's successful beginning I expected

it to fail through lack of support as the magazine, the debating society and the outing to Linlithgow had failed, so I was surprised to find after three months that enthusiasm was increasing. The Students' Representative Council was packed with members of the tunnel committee and continually organised dances to pay for the installation of more powerful machinery. A sort of tension became obvious throughout the building. People jumped at small sounds, laughed at feeble jokes and quarrelled without provocation. Perhaps they unconsciously feared the tunnel would open a volcanic vent, though things like increase of temperature, water seepage and the presence of gas had been so far absent. Sometimes I wondered how the project remained free from interference. An engineering venture supported by several hundred people can hardly be called a secret. It was natural for those outside the school to regard rumours as fantastic inventions, but why did none of the teachers interfere? Only a minority were active supporters of the project; two were being bribed to remain silent. I am sure the director and deputy director did not know, but what about the rest who knew and said nothing? Perhaps they also regarded the tunnel as a possible means of escape.

One day work on the tunnel stopped. The first shift going to work in the morning coffee-break discovered that the basement entrance was locked. There were several tunnel entrances now, but all were found to be locked, and since the tunnel committee had vanished it was assumed they were inside. This caused a deal of speculation.

I have always kept clear of mass movements, so on meeting the president of the committee in a lonely upper corridor one evening I said, 'Hullo, Mildred,' and would have passed on, but she gripped my arm and said, 'Come with me.'

She led me a few yards to the open door of what I had thought was a disused service lift. She said, 'You'd better sit on the floor,' and closed the gates behind us and pulled a lever. The lift fell like a stone with a noise so high-pitched that it was sometimes inaudible. After fifteen minutes it decelerated in violent jerks, then stopped. Mildred opened the gates and we stepped out.

In spite of myself I was impressed by what I saw. We stood in a corridor with an arched ceiling, asphalt floors and walls of white tile. It swept left and right in a curve that prevented seeing more than a mile in each direction. 'Very good,' I said, 'very good indeed. How did you manage it? The fluorescent lighting alone must have cost a fortune.'

Mildred said gloomily, 'We didn't make this place; we only reached it.'

At that moment an elderly man passed us on a bicycle. He wore a peaked cap, an armband with some kind of badge on it and was otherwise naked, for the air was warm. As he passed he raised a hand in a friendly gesture. I said, 'Who was that?'

'Some kind of official. There aren't many of them on this level.'

'How many levels are there?'

'Three. This one has dormitories and canteens for the staff, and underneath are the offices of the administration, and under that is the engine.'

'What engine?'

'The one that drives us round the sun.'

'But *gravity* drives the world round the sun.'

'Has anyone ever told you what gravity is and how it operates?'

I realised nobody ever had. Mildred said, 'Gravity is nothing but a word top-level scientists use to hide their ignorance.'

I asked her how the engine was powered. She said, 'Steam.'

'Not nuclear fission?'

'No, the industrial design boys are quite certain it's a steam engine of the most primitive sort imaginable. They're down there measuring and sketching with the rest of the commit-tee. We'll show you a picture in a day or two.'

'Does nobody ask what right you have to go poking about

inside this thing?'

'No. It's like all big organisations. The staff are so numerous that you can go where you like if you look confident enough.'

I had to meet a friend in half an hour so we got into the lift and started back up. I said, 'Well, Mildred, it's interesting of course, but I don't know why you brought me to see it.'

She said, 'I'm worried. The others keep laughing at the machinery and discussing how to alter it. They think we can inprove the climate by taking us nearer the sun. I'm afraid we're doing wrong.'

'Of course you're doing wrong! You're supposed to be studying art, not planetary motion. I would never have suggested the project if I'd thought you would take it to this length.'

She let me out on the ground floor saying, 'We can't turn back now.' Then I suppose she redescended, for I never saw her again.

That night I was awakened by an explosion and my bed falling heavily to the ceiling. The sun, which had just set, came up again. The city was inundated by sea. We survivors crouched a long time among ruins threatened by earthquakes, avalanches and whirlwinds. All clocks were working at different speeds and the sun, after reaching the height of noon, stayed there. At length the elements calmed and we examined the new situation. It is clear that the planet has broken into several bits. Our bit is not revolving. To enjoy starlight and darkness, to get a good night's sleep, we have to walk to the other side of our new world, a journey of several miles, with an equally long journey back when we want daylight.

It will be hard to remake life on the old basis. Sometimes I look across the very near horizon at other chunks of the old globe. It seems likely that the accident resulted from a chance remark of mine. It will teach me to keep my mouth shut, in future.

Donald Malcolm has published numerous short stories and two novels, The Unknown Shore *and* The Iron Rain *(Laser, 1976). He too wears a non-fiction hat as a writer on astronomy and philately. Several of his stories were set in the DREAM research institute and here we have an unpublished example, specially revised for this anthology.*

Donald Malcolm
FOR SOME DARK PURPOSE

"It seems to me I am trying to tell you a dream – making a vain attempt, because no relation of a dream can convey the dream-sensation, that commingling of absurdity, surprise and bewilderment in a tremor of struggling revolt, that notion of being captured by the incredible which is of the very essence of dreams."

Joseph Conrad, Heart of Darkness

THE BRASSY GONG OF THE SUN BEAT OUT WAVES OF heat into the stifled air and shadows sprawled in the streets like great inky dogs. The trees along the avenue were limp, like the banners of a surrendered army. August in London could be hot and uncomfortable.

Conrad's words seemed for Maxwell to sum up the challenges of work at the Dream Research Establishment, and they passed through his mind once again as he approached the building. He reached the front entrance as McLean was coming out. They regarded each other – as usual – with wary hostility.

'Good morning, Dr Maxwell.' McLean's bow was exaggerated; his eyes, when he straightened, cold and flint-like.

The Director of DREAM acknowledged his departing research-subject curtly, holding back the annoyance and frustration produced by contact with McLean. Similar feelings had been building up in the other members of Maxwell's staff who had been working with the man who was the most gifted – and at the same time the rudest and most arrogant – person that they had ever been able to study.

For a start, McLean had been displaying mathematical skill that appeared to border on the uncanny. And his talents seemed to extend much further than that. Already, in the brief two weeks he had spent with them, they suspected that McLean had somehow established a kind of telepathic communication with the mainframe computer at the London Computing Centre, and used it for some purpose of his own which was not at all clear. That was the explanation that had developed for a series of persistent problems with the computer which had kept producing fragmentary references to DREAM in its output.

Now it was all over. From a purely personal point of view, Maxwell felt relieved. Objectively, he knew that McLean was leaving just as he was beginning to get really interesting.

'Why don't you stay on, or if you feel that you want a break, come back later? We still have a lot to learn from you.'

McLean said disparagingly: 'There's nothing *I* can learn from *you,* though. I got what I wanted.'

He gave Maxwell a mock salute and was off along the pavement, taking care to step on all the lines and cracks, just as a child would do.

'Some child,' Maxwell muttered as he turned round abruptly and collided with Duncan Livingstone, DREAM's psychologist.

'McLean,' he said by way of explanation as they went to his office, and that was explanation enough.

'He's a fascinating and mysterious young man,' his colleague said. 'Usually, I manage to get to know people very well in two weeks. I didn't get remotely close to McLean. Or get below the surface of that aggressive outward personality.'

Maxwell grimaced, as John, the night maintenance engineer, knocked and brought in two mugs of tea. 'No problems last night, Dr Maxwell. The trouble seems to be over.'

When he had gone, Livingstone said, 'So have we really seen the last of McLean?'

'It seems like it. But who was the real McLean? When he

came here, he was cheaply dressed, untidy, surly and sly. Within a few days he had expensive clothes, discreet jewellery, money, and radiated confidence and arrogance. How do we account for that?'

The psychologist tapped his mug. 'I think he did find a way to tap into the big computer at the Centre. And as a result his mathematical skills have been somehow sharpened and amplified by the contact. The money could have come from using those skills in pseudo-predictive fields: horses, dogs, gambling – anything that would give an instant return. He probably raised it to the level of a science.'

Maxwell drew a breath. 'If he was doing that – was he predicting things? Or *influencing* them?'

'I don't know. I'm surmising, that's all.'

'Was there anything unusual on McLean's tapes last night?'

'Nothing. His activity was normal. His dream periods fell on the average times, and the dreams themselves were commonplace, quite unlike before.'

Maxwell leafed through the reports, leaving the main details for further study. 'He comes to us, apparently ordinary and lazy, looking for a place where he can get some money and keep himself as far as possible from work. He has incredible dreams, full of mathematical gobbledegook, almost wrecks the London Centre's computer, and then, on his last night – nothing. It's as if he were winding down here, preparing to move on to something else.'

He closed the file firmly as Livingstone said, 'I know less about him now than I did two weeks ago.'

Michael, the day maintenance engineer, put his head round the door. 'Number Four EEG unit has just failed, Dr Maxwell. I'll let you know as soon as it's repaired.'

MAXWELL SAT IN HIS OFFICE, thinking about the progress that had been made in the years since research into dreaming had been started at the University of Chicago in 1953.

There were now forty-three Dream Research Establishments, popularly known as DREAMs. Most of the work took place in the small hours, and someone cheerfully tagged AM on to DRE. London was the third-largest establishment.

Dreaming had been recognised for a long time to be a process as natural as breathing, occupying about twenty percent of sleeping time. If someone was deprived of sleep – and hence, of dreaming – then there was deterioration of health, physical and mental. One theory held that so-called day-dreaming was an attempt by the mind to make up the deficiency. And there was a relation between actions in dreams and in real life.

Observation of the rapid eye movements made in dreaming – the so-called REMs – showed that actions took the same time to perform in dreams as they did in waking life.

Using these same rapid eye movements, the times and durations of dreams had been analysed, until the sequence of a night's dreaming could be displayed as a line on a jagged graph.

Dreaming had been shown to occur several times in a night, but only at particular stages of sleep. The first dream occurs during the drift into sleep, and it is fragmentary, transitory and disconnected, as if a moving film were blocked off at random. The plunge into the deepest sleep is sudden, like stepping off a mental precipice. This period lasts about thirty minutes. The sleeper then approaches the lightest phase of sleep, reached just over an hour after falling asleep. On average, the sleeper remains in this stage for nine minutes, and during this time has the first organised dream. Then comes a sleep not quite as deep as the first thirty-minute period. Dream passages follow at intervals until the final dream, which lasts till awakening.

Maxwell's institute took in its research-subjects for two weeks at a time – enough usually for about seventy dreams apiece. In an effort to unravel the allegories and symbols of each person's dreams, the first step was to have a personality pattern drawn up by a psychologist. The graph of each person's sleep was followed each night, and correlated with the data from all the subjects at all forty-three establishments.

He turned to look at the filing cabinet where the data on the 'M's was kept, just as Dr Toni Smith, darkly-attractive and elegant, on a year's secondment from Chicago, came in with a heavy sheaf of data sheets for his desk.

'Something to keep you from getting bored,' she said.

MAXWELL HAD ONLY BEEN a few hours in Rome, on the last stop of a December tour of other research establishments, when a telephone call came for him. It was Duncan Livingstone.

'McLean has turned up, Edward. And in very odd circumstances. He was found, apparently in a coma, and taken to hospital. That was two days ago. He awakened briefly about 6 pm.'

Maxwell gazed out at the bright Italian sunlight, and felt the day clouding over.

Duncan went on: 'He said, "Must tell Maxwell. Dream. Many layers of darkness." The duty nurse heard him and was sharp enough to pass the message on. He had no identification on him when he was found. The hospital called the police again, and they came here. They want you to come back at once.'

'What can I do? I'm not a relative.'

Livingstone knew that Maxwell was intrigued and he pressed on. 'He asked for *you,* Edward.'

Maxwell, in the land where Horatius once held the bridge, tried to make a last stand.

'Damn it, you know I have more to do on this visit. I can't really leave yet.'

'I'll meet you here.'

AS SOON AS HE SAW DUNCAN, Maxwell knew that something was badly wrong.

'McLean's gone.'

Maxwell hadn't even been home, and he dumped his cases in a corner. He kept his coat on, and puddles quickly formed on the floor.

'How? When?' He felt far from the sunshine of Rome.

'About two hours ago. No one knew anything about his disappearance, apparently. He simply put on his clothes and walked out.'

'Just like that? After a coma? With hospital staff round about – what did the duty nurse, other staff, say.'

Duncan had been percolating coffee, and he pushed a mug across the desk.

'Now we come to the puzzling part. There was a nurse on duty, of course. But she swears that she did not leave the room during her spell of duty, nor did she fall asleep.'

'And no one believes the poor girl.' Maxwell sipped his drink. 'She's in trouble, and no fault of hers, I'll bet.'

The psychologist put on his hat, scarf and coat. 'We'll see Dr Armour there. He's on her side, says she's truthful, reliable and efficient – and can't understand what happened.'

Dr Armour was tall, fair-haired, built like a caber-tosser, and looked about thirty-five, though it became clear that he was somewhat older.

'McLean was originally found in an alley, about half a mile from DREAM, sitting on a packing-case. The shopkeeper who found him said that his eyes were open and staring. He wasn't dirty or injured, so he hadn't been mugged. The shop-keeper called the police, who brought him here. The only time that he spoke was to say, "Must tell Maxwell. Dream. Many layers of darkness." The nurse had heard of you and your work through reading articles and seeing you on television. She told me. I told the police and they arrived on Dr Livingstone's doorstep.'

Maxwell was conscious of sodden trousers clinging icily to his legs. McLean had obviously been trying, for whatever reason, to get back in touch with DREAM when something happened to him.

'You said that McLean had no injuries, Dr Armour. Did you find out what was wrong with him?'

'In laymen's terms, I'd say nervous exhaustion. A build-up of at least several weeks. But what's this about? It must be important to make you hurry back from Rome.'

Maxwell had already decided that there was no point in involving the doctor and his staff any deeper than they had to be, and noticed that Armour was watching him with frank scrutiny.

'I don't know myself what's happening.' That was the truth. 'When McLean was last at DREAM, he left rather abruptly, without giving us time to finish our research with him. Naturally, I'm anxious to know why he's come back, asking for me, only to disappear again.' That was being economical with the truth.

The doctor looked unconvinced, but he was astute enough to know that he wasn't going to get an answer, perhaps because Maxwell couldn't give it to him. He reached into a pocket and brought out some news-clippings.

'Maybe these will help. They were in his pocket-book.' He passed them across the desk as he rose, adding, 'I'll have to get back on duty, now, if there's nothing else.'

He scribbled a few words on a piece of paper as Maxwell took the cuttings, and handed it over. 'The names of the doctor and the policeman who were here last night, in case you need them.'

MAXWELL PUSHED BACK the plates and the remains of the late dinner that his wife had found herself undertaking at even shorter notice than usual. He moved away the cheeseboard from between him and Duncan, and spread out the newspaper cuttings.

There were twenty or thirty in all, many of them little more than snippets. *CHILDREN SAVED FROM CANAL: rescuer not traced. SUICIDE PREVENTED: mystery warning given to police. RAILWAY DISASTER AVERTED: who switched the points?*

Silently they read the reports of rescue from all manner of violent and unpleasant death.

Livingstone was suddenly excited.

'Look at this one, Edward!'

Maxwell took the cutting. *COMPUTER ACCIDENTS AT JODRELL BANK: police probe, sabotage suspected.* All the accidents, fortunately minor, had started about three months ago. The footnote by the *Guardian* science editor was even more interesting. The radio telescope had been picking up random signals for three months. This was not confirmed by Jodrell Bank. It wasn't known if the signals were coming from unannounced American or Russian satellites, or interplanetary probes, and both countries denied knowledge of any source transmitting over that period of time.

'McLean,' Maxwell said. 'I wonder if he knows – '

'I'm beginning not to like this, Edward. He's been the mystery rescuer mentioned in all those cuttings, or in at least the bigger percentage of them. And if he was able to tamper with the London computer before, he would be just as able to use the Jodrell Bank one now.'

Maxwell put the cutting in a file. 'We'll chart the dates of these tomorrow. We can't be sure at this stage if there is any connection between the rescues, the accidents and the signals, but it's possible there could be a pattern.'

He helped Duncan on with his coat. 'If only they had managed to hold on to McLean until I got there – ' and realised that he had managed to make the psychologist smile for the first time that evening.

THE NEXT DAY was as bright as a newly-struck coin, and the air was brittle with cold. As he walked to work, his heels clicking sharply on the early-morning pavements, Maxwell thought about McLean. He was certain that McLean was involved in the rescues. And he was just as certain that McLean was evil. McLean had used the London computer for some dark purpose. Now he had moved on to the next stage of his plans. He had to be found and stopped. Almost, Maxwell found himself thinking, *destroyed.* And yet, he mused, McLean had wanted to contact him, had desperately wanted to get a message through to him. Why?

Duncan was at the establishment and had already taken the report of the duty doctor. Autumn and winter were busy times at DREAM and there were always full complements of research-subjects. He nodded to several strangers in the building.

'Is there anything in the duty doctor's report, Duncan?'

The psychologist had had a large table brought into Maxwell's office. Above the table, pinned to the wall, was a large fold-out map of London Postal Districts and parts of the surrounding counties. He activated a tape-recorder, saying, 'Listen to this.'

Maxwell ignored the preliminary information about the research-subject, her identity-number, the time and the duration of the dream. The tape went on:

'I was driving a red car up a steep hill. But I can't drive, and although I can't tell one pedal from another, the car drove on. I had to weave between other parked cars. A bright yellow car, its headlights blazing, came racing down the hill and I thought there was going to be a collision. Somehow, my car stopped, and I threw my arm across my face. When I looked again, the yellow car had gone and everything was in darkness, no lights in any of the houses, nothing.

'The car started to move again of its own accord. Suddenly vehicles appeared from the cul-de-sacs at the top of the hill, a brightly-lit bus from the right, a van from the left, and they charged down the hill, side by side, towards me. The headlights blinded me, then they were gone.

'At the top of the hill stood a hideous figure, outlined by some kind of cold fire. The head was intact, although it seemed to have no eyes, but the body was horribly wasted. The car was still moving, but it didn't seem to get any nearer the figure. A vague shape began to swell behind the figure until it filled the sky ... menacing ... evil beyond belief ... '

Duncan said, 'We had a wee bit of trouble calming her down, after that dream. Fortunately, she's very stable. We didn't let her carry on last night, but she says she'll be back tonight.'

'Is she in any danger, do you think?'

Livingstone brought a file over and sat in front of Maxwell's desk.

'I think her mind is safe enough. That was more than a grisly nightmare that she had. Someone was trying to send a message *here,* not to her. You'll recall that McLean said, "Must tell Maxwell. DREAM. Many layers of darkness." He left the hospital before he could tell you anything. Maybe he had to leave. He could be trying to tell you now.'

'A presentiment of evil,' Maxwell said. 'I was thinking about that on my way here this morning. The nightmare tells us nothing that we can interpret with certainty. Maybe the cuttings could lead us somewhere – '

'There's something else.'

Maxwell, about to get up from his seat, stopped. 'More?'

'The research-subject – Miss Fry – was talking to me last night. For the past two months, she has been receiving impressions, mainly formless, during the day. It was like having a television image flickering at the edge of vision. One day she was impelled to leave the shop where she works and go outside – just in time to prevent an old man from walking into the path of a taxi. She got the hint of a name. Ela? Atman?'

Maxwell looked thoughtful. 'Another unexpected rescue.' Going over to the table, he started to spread out the cuttings. 'I called the police last night. They admitted that the circumstances of McLean's arrival and departure were peculiar, but as he hadn't committed a crime they would take no action. They were right about things being peculiar. McLean is our problem.'

He finished laying out the cuttings in date order, twenty-seven in all. Livingstone tabulated them by PLACE and DATE. Then, using coloured pencils, they marked the locations of the incidents as near as they could on the approximate spots on the map. Maxwell had divided the cuttings into three groups and they could see the pattern emerging as they worked. When they had finished, they stood back to survey the results.

Group One comprised four rescues which had taken place in Clapham during the last twelve days of August. The second sequence involved eleven incidents which had occurred in areas such as Paddington, Deptford, Sydenham, Wimbledon and Barnes, over a period of five weeks. The remaining twelve incidents had happened over a large area, in five cases at locations between forty and fifty miles from the source of the original four. The last incident was dated two weeks previously.

'You see where that one is, Duncan,' Maxwell said, pointing to a smaller map of South England and Wales. 'Carlton, near Shoeburyness, McLean's birthplace. That seems to remove any doubts about his involvement.'

'Yes.'

'And the man who was rescued was the local headmaster – who would have been from the school McLean went to. His name's Dix – I've met him. It says here he was beachcasting just after dusk, slipped on a rock, cracked his head open, wakened up in hospital and didn't know how he got there. He had a thirteen pound bass on his line.'

'There's plenty of information in these few provincial cuttings, in contrast to the meagre offerings from London. This kind of story is always going to be swamped by bigger ones in the city.'

Maxwell tapped a pencil on this teeth. 'We're left with a number of unanswered questions. Why has McLean stopped whatever it was he was doing? It there any connection between him and those mysterious unconfirmed signals from space? And why go up to Cheshire to tinker with a computer at Jodrell Bank? There's been no dramatic rescue in that area.'

He paused, then added, 'But we could find out more about Jodrell Bank and its computer from Jason Brown at the London Computing Centre – he'll have contacts there. He might be able to get us information about the signals as well. And about any computer deviations at other places.'

Duncan said, 'I know a journalist with a lot of contacts in Scottish and provincial papers. He could be able to supply us with reports and seemingly fortuitous rescues, the kind that won't make the nationals, especially not in these times.'

'It's worth a try, Duncan. McLean's radius of action has been widening – '

He broke off and snapped the pencil. 'We've been miss-ing something obvious. If we had stopped to think about it, how could McLean be directly responsible for all the rescues? It wouldn't be physically possible.'

He paused again, driving his fist into his palm.

'Miss Fry.'

Livingstone stared at Maxwell for a moment.

'Of course! Miss Fry. She is receptive. But low grade, because McLean was unable to get a clear signal to her. All she picked up were vague impressions, except in the case where she saved the man. So we have to conjecture a network of receptive minds, being built up and used by McLean. Does that seem reasonable?'

'Yes. But I wish I knew why he's doing it. Kindness to his fellow men is hardly one of his traits.'

They parted, Maxwell to get on with the day's business, Duncan to go north to see three people: a small boy with strange powers; a friendly journalist; and a lady about a satellite.

That evening, Miss Fry, and several other people, died in a fire which started in the single room of a partially-crippled pensioner, whose cat knocked over a candle during a power cut.

DUNCAN LIVINGSTONE was comfortably settled in a deep leather armchair in the reading room of the Glasgow University Union. He was rounding off an excellent lunch with coffee. Sheila Kirn, seated opposite, was an astronomer at the University, where she had originally gone to study literature, and had worked for a time on a study of allegory in medieval Scottish poetry. A long-standing interest in mathematics eventually won through and took her into the study of planetary motion, but it was usually a short step for her to take from the faraway worlds of space to those of the imagination.

'Sheila – do you recall the case of Sammy Kinloch, about two years ago?'

'Yes.' Her green eyes narrowed at the memory. 'I could

hardly forget him. It was a pity that his apparent telepathic power disappeared so quickly.'

Something in Livingstone's expression made her ask, 'It did fade out, didn't it?'

Duncan nodded. 'It did. But the power, or something akin to it, has returned.'

She sipped the coffee and waited for him to continue.

'I've been looking for people who might be particularly receptive to telepathic messages, just like Sammy seemed to be able to do. I thought that his ability was so strong at its peak that it might be worth going to see him now. And it was. It's come back, and now it's not merely messages. Sammy's seeing pictures in his head. The places are as clear as if he was looking at them visually. Once or twice he recognised the scenes.'

She loosened her long dark hair on her shoulders. 'How can I help?'

'Sammy says he sees the pictures at certain times of day. About every hour and a half. I sat with him most of the day and tried to time it exactly, from the start of the pictures and their duration. There really is a regular pattern to them, a very regular pattern. The timing's not just to the hour, but to the minute – every 89.1 minutes, in fact.'

She looked carefully at him. 'As regularly as a satellite passing overhead?'

'Exactly – just as regular as a satellite. And the pictures arrive, and seem to him to be showing him somewhere that he ought to go to. He doesn't know why – just that it's very important that he goes to the place in the pictures, right away.'

'He feels someone's trying to influence him?'

'Precisely. So I'd like to know if there is a satellite fitting the orbital period and the timings.'

Sheila's office was tidy, with star charts on one wall and a satellite photograph of Islay on another. The view from the sky showed the detail of the hills and moorland, and even the houses of Port Ellen. She ran her finger over each line of the tables as she checked them through.

'There's nothing with an orbital period of 89.1 minutes that passes over this part of Scotland. Nothing in here, anyway.'

She paused.

'But we have had some anomalies in a current study we're doing, which involves taking a series of photographs of a sector of sky overhead.'

Duncan held back the question and let her continue.

'We're looking for near-Earth asteroids, comparing each photograph with the next for movement. Satellites in high orbits move at similar angular rates to our 'targets', so the computer eliminates all of the known satellites. But there's one object that's moving so rapidly that it has to be close to earth – like a satellite. But since it's not on the published records, and since no new launch had been announced, it can't be one of the usual ones, for weather or communications. We thought it might be a bit of a sensitive subject to get involved in,'

'Could it be just a spy satellite, or could it be big enough to have a man on board?'

'Either, I suppose.'

As they left the Astronomy Department in University Gardens, she said, 'But why would anyone in a satellite want to influence the routine pattern of people's daily lives down here?'

The evening traffic was lighter than usual as they drove across Byres Road, parking outside a block of flats in Downiebrae Road opposite.

They had arrived at the top of the second flight of stairs when a small figure burst past them.

'Sammy – !'

The boy didn't answer, and kept on going. They scrambled after him.

WHEN MAXWELL ARRIVED at the Computing Centre, Jason Brown had the appearance of an avalanche waiting for someone to fall on.

'Edward! You've certainly started something!' he said, nostrils flaring and eyes even brighter than usual. Maxwell cleared himself a space among the papers strewn everywhere as the Director continued, 'I've gathered reports from many places, from people with computers of all types and sizes. Haven't you found McLean, yet?'

'No. Can you detect any pattern?'

'You're expecting a lot in a short time,' Brown said, still pacing. 'There's interference on a grand scale. And it's been growing – rapidly. If it is McLean behind it all, his mind must have become very powerful indeed. Very powerful.'

'Is there any connection between what's happening and the stories of strange signals received at Jodrell Bank?'

'I don't know. I can't find out a thing.'

Maxwell was disappointed, but didn't comment directly. 'We have two patterns of unusual events, and both seem to focus on McLean. On the one hand we have these computer malfunctions, and we know that he seems to have the power to somehow tap into these machines and use them for his own purposes. What those purposes are isn't completely clear, although we know that while he was with us – and almost certainly tapping into your own computer – he became in a matter of days much wealthier and much more self-assured. It's as if he had a latent power that he discovered while with us: from out below the outer layer of his personality another McLean emerged, confident, powerful, knowing what he wanted and able to get it.'

Jason had sat down. 'So he used his skill with our computer to make money – working out gambling patterns or just extracting data and selling it. And he's doing the same with the others.'

'That's possible. But the other pattern of events that he's somehow at the centre of doesn't square with that. There seem to have been a remarkable series of rescues, where people have been saved from accidents by someone calling onto the scene just in time. Not necessarily McLean himself, but someone who's in some way influenced by him – apparently telepathically. And building up into some kind of network.'

'Many people have wanted to avert tragedies that go on

around them. Now that McLean has the power to do so, he's doing what we all have often desperately wished we could do.'

'But that's just the point,' Maxwell declared. 'If it was anyone else, you might believe it. But not McLean. He's cold, arrogant, self-centred. I've been going back into his past, asking people who knew him before. I phoned his old headmaster, Dix. His first words were "Still in trouble?" He thought that McLean at school had the makings of a mathematical genius. But he always used his talent for petty ends. And always – totally – for himself.'

Jason tried a shot. 'So you think that something happened to change him? Some strong influence that he came under that affected him so strongly that he began to do things that were alien to his nature?'

Maxwell had to admit that that was pretty well on target. 'It is possible,' he accepted, 'that McLean through his interfering with computers and electronic equipment – or simply through his growing telepathic ability – has somehow contacted, or been contacted by, an alien presence. And maybe this alien presence is, somehow, making him do – for perhaps the first time in his life – some good in the world. As a sort of alien agent for good.'

Jason looked at him closely. 'But you don't believe that?'

'I'm not sure that I do. You see, it wouldn't quite explain what happened when he fell into a coma. Oh yes, the coma itself could be explained by the clash of wills between McLean and the alien force. He'd never like doing anything anyone else wanted him to do, and particularly not if it involved the benefit of other people. So he could have become exhausted with the effort to fight it.'

'But – ?'

'But it doesn't explain why he wanted so desperately to get a message to me. A message with the words "many layers of darkness". Not me. Not from McLean.'

'So you think that there may be some dark purpose behind the way that McLean and his telepathic network are building up.'

Maxwell was forced to agree that he did. 'I thought at first

M

that McLean had contacted something which he was using for his own ends. But now it may be the other way round.'

'But it may be a force for good. It could be gradually looking for suitable people and building the right ones into a network for good. It could even be hope for the human race, to bring us all together.'

Maxwell thought about Miss Fry, but didn't take up the point. The telephone rang. Jason lifted the receiver, listened, and handed it to Maxwell, 'Duncan.'

In turn, Maxwell listened, saying nothing. When he replaced the received, he looked older.

'It's much worse than we thought, Most of the rescues seem to have been countered by accidents, with many deaths.'

DUNCAN AND SHEILA reached the street again. By following the direction in which so many heads were turned, they knew that Sammy was going to Great Western Road. A squeal of brakes and raised voices confirmed that. Duncan ran on to the street and went after Sammy, bumping his way forward. Fighting his way through the human confetti that eddied and swirled colourfully in Byres Road would not be easy. Suddenly a pram rammed him and he toppled heavily to the pavement.

Meanwhile Elaine Bateman was half-walking, half-running, along Queen Margaret Drive, past the BBC, towards the junction with Great Western Road, opposite Byres Road. She had a vague picture in her mind about an accident, and she felt she had to go there. She did not understand the compulsion and she was frightened, but she felt unable to stop herself. She ran between a car and a heavy lorry, throught the taxi rank and then across more traffic to reach the pavement outside the Botanic Gardens. She dropped her handbag and seemed oblivious to the shouts behind her. She would soon be at the corner with Byres Road. The noise of the traffic was like that of a tank division on the move.

Sammy was almost at Great Western Road. He had crossed the street, to be nearer Queen Margaret Drive. He had not much time.

They saw each other at the same instant and began to run, shouting, unheard in the din.

The traffic on both sides started to move on the amber light. Sammy caused two fast-accelerating cars to brake hard and they skidded on the greasy surface. A tanker lumbering behind also braked and slewed across the junction into the path of a city-bound bus, and kept on going, swinging the bus round and over on its side, on top of the baker's van coming up the inside lane. It was all over in twenty seconds.

The boy and the woman, unhurt, stood staring, each at the person they had come to rescue. Their minds meshed and they *knew* …

DUNCAN HAD FINISHED a long telephone call to Maxwell. He leaned wearily back into the largest armchair in Sheila's flat and wished that he could think of a good enough excuse to avoid the drive to the station and the night train back to London. Sheila poured him a final glass.

'Is there really no way whether you can tell if it was a real accident, caused by confusion – or a complicated malevolent plan?'

'It could be either. These accidents seem to go hand-in-hand with real rescues – or with people trying to carry out a rescue but not succeeding. This time it could be real confusion – both Sammy and Mrs Bateman are telepathic. I knew her face when I saw her, and now I remember where I've seen her before. She was one of our subjects at the DREAM institute a while ago. About six years back. And very good too. She has undoubted ability to receive the kind of pictures in her mind that Sammy's been getting.'

'So could they both have picked up the same message?'

'It's possible. And maybe by doing so, they caused the very thing that they were trying to avoid. That's what will haunt them now. But it could be instead that someone – or something – is in some way testing them out, probing their minds, seeing how they react. I just don't know.'

'So the messages from space – if that's where they're coming from – could be for a good purpose, or they could be for a much darker one.'

'That,' said Duncan, 'is about the height of it.'

THE MORNING WAS DAMP AND GREY, and the drive from the station had been through roads where wet slush still lay, but at least the coffee in the pot was strong and black. Duncan had gone over the full story of his Glasgow visit again, and Maxwell's concluding question had hung once again in the air, unanswered.

'McLean's built up a network of minds, but is it McLean who's running it?'

Dr Toni Smith knocked and entered. 'I've checked Mrs Bateman's records from the time she was with us, and you were right. She showed strong telepathic abilities. And,' she added, 'there's a policeman here to see you.'

The policeman turned out to be a tall, alert, young man, whose well-groomed appearance made him seem more like a City gent. *Heavens*, thought Maxwell, *a yuppie policeman.*

'Sergeant Don Mayes, sir. Dr Armour mentioned your name. We want your help with a formal identification. If you wouldn't mind.'

'Identification – ?' The word hung in the air.

'Yes, Dr Maxwell. The man has been dead for at least two weeks, maybe longer.'

As they pulled on their overcoats and went to the car, Maxwell asked, 'Where did you find him?'

Mayes said, 'In an old house, not far from here. Demolition workers found him.'

They reached the mortuary. Dr Bryant, the police surgeon, said, 'A most peculiar case. The body showed the usual signs of decay, but the head and brain were wholly preserved. I can't understand it.'

Behind his back, horror sparked between Maxwell and Livingstone.

Miss Fry's dream!

The room seemed to get even colder as Bryant drew out a cabinet and uncovered the cadaver. Then even he stared in disbelief. McLean's head was now in the same advanced state as the body.

After what seemed to Maxwell the longest few seconds he had ever known, Bryant covered up the body and closed the cabinet. They returned to the office, no one quite sure what to say. The policeman broke the uneasy silence.

'I have to write up a report for my Inspector, including the formal identification. Dr Maxwell – can you identify the body as McLean's?'

Maxwell did not envy the policeman his apparent coolness. He was trying to shake the vision out of his mind.

'No, I can't. Maybe dental records will help. We have a few details of his birthplace and background on file, and maybe you can trace a dentist through that. I'll have them sent round.'

'Thank you, sir. We may want to see you again.'

Maxwell nodded, and shook hands before leaving. He could feel Bryant in particular watching him as he walked to the door, but no final question came as he went out into the grey drizzle of the street.

In the car, Duncan said, 'We've got an answer now to your own question, haven't we? About who's running the network of minds that McLean has patiently been building up?'

Maxwell couldn't think of anything to say, and waited for him to continue.

'The answer,' said Duncan, 'is that it's not McLean.' He paused. 'But someone – or *something* – has been controlling it *through* McLean for the past fortnight.' He paused again. 'But isn't any more.'

Maxwell thought back to the sequence of events that had led McLean to collapse into a coma and then make an apparently remarkable recovery from hospital. And McLean's message – McLean's *last* message. "Many layers of darkness." They were probing the surface of the upper layer, the one that McLean had become ensnared in, but now their lead through him was gone, and they were as far away as ever from the attempt to delineate the dark.

But the network remained. The network built up by McLean. No longer run through him, but waiting to be activated.

Maxwell sat up straight. 'The small research unit we have in Glasgow – your two telepathic contacts there – drive as fast as you possibly can to Heathrow – right away. We'll phone from the airport.'

A flurry of grey sleet broke on the windscreen as they accelerated onto the motorway.

THE FIVE PEOPLE were in a room at the DREAM unit in St Vincent Street: Maxwell, Livingstone, Sheila Kirn, Sammy and Elaine Bateman.

Maxwell said, 'You both realise that this power that you have has become dangerous. Something alien is influencing your minds. It kept McLean's mind alive for over two weeks after he should have been dead. It overcame him and used him to build up extensions in a network – of minds like yours. People were picked up and drawn in, or dropped out if they weren't suitable.'

They listened without interruption as he continued.

'The force seems to be … resting … just now. Neither of you has been affected since the accident. And it seems to have simply dropped its control over McLean. We want to take the opportunity to try and break its influence over the network and we think that you might be able to do that – especially you, Sammy.'

The boy sat very quietly and didn't move.

'You seem to have a strong connection with other minds, Sammy. We want you and Mrs Bateman to try and contact someone in the network, and ask them, in turn, to forge a link with others. The idea is to form a single mind, a gestalt, to repel the intruder.'

Maxwell paused for a moment. 'The one final thing that

I should say is that this now may well be our only contact with this alien force. If it consolidates its hold over the network, it may be impossible for us ever to drive it away. So whatever happens today, however hard the going may get, you must not under any circumstances at all give way. For the sake of all of us.'

They were taken to one of the rooms normally used by research-subjects during dreaming sessions.

'We'll leave you alone, for you know best what you have to do. If you want anything, the microphones are live.'

Research-subjects were usually monitored on closed-circuit television, but there were windows for direct observation, if required. For several minutes, nothing happened. Then Mrs Bateman said, 'I've picked up somebody in Aberdeen … '

Almost immediately Sammy exclaimed, 'Carlisle – a woman – strong contact … '

Livingstone, with his passion for maps, had put a large-scale one of Britain on a board, and the place was like a war operations room as he used coloured tacks to chart the progress of the link-up.

Maxwell said, 'I think the network will get stronger as more minds come into it. The more powerful minds will reinforce the weaker ones. I wonder if the alien force is aware of what's happening?'

Elaine Bateman's voice cut off any reply Duncan might have made.

'The man in Aberdeen says he's picked up a contact from much further north. I think it's in Reykjavik.'

'So the network is not confined to Britain. I suspected as much,' Livingstone said.

He pulled over a blackboard and, producing a map of the world, pinned that up.

Within two hours, his coloured tacks were spread widely over it.

AS THE TIME WENT ON, it was clear that the network was developing into a unity of its own, with messages flowing backwards and forwards around the component minds. To the watchers through the window of the control-room, there were only Sammy and Elaine Bateman in direct view, each lying on a cot normally used for dream-research subjects. In one way, thought Maxwell, it was as if the two were indeed dreaming, eyes closed and unmoving, stirring occasionally as a wave of thought drifted across the global mind that they had become part of. The earlier comments of recognition had stopped, as the new members of the network had been greeted and settled into the flow of overall thought.

It seemed, from the outside viewing-window, that several of the individual minds in the network were more powerful than the rest; seven, including Sammy. They seemed to be forging the net closer together, gathering up fainter or more scattered thoughts and amplifying them, to flow onwards with renewed strength. To Duncan, his overall chart now apparently complete, it was as if these stronger minds were acting as the foci of all the energy contained in the system, the energy that would have to be turned against the alien force. He thought of static electricity building up in a massive accumulator, ready for a sudden intense discharge in a lightning bolt of concentrated energy. Idly, in the stillness that prevailed, he plotted the locations of the seven centres of power, and began to join up the lines.

Sammy cried out, fracturing the silence.

'I CAN'T DESCRIBE IT in any kind of words,' said Elaine Bateman. 'Evil doesn't fit. Evil – goodness – justice … these are human concepts and mean nothing to it. It's certainly intelligent … but in a different way from us. I had a feeling of – darkness, a massive source of sentient darkness – many layers of darkness – trying to control our minds.'

Many layers of darkness. Maxwell thought of McLean.

Elaine's words were beginning to slur as sudden, heavy, tiredness set in.

'I – we – don't think that its influence was either good or bad. It was – trying to make contact. It wanted to contact us. I don't know why the accidents occurred. Maybe its messages weren't coming through properly. They went to the wrong places … took the wrong forms … and upset balances. Things were disturbed … and went the wrong way.'

There was a long pause, and then Sammy spoke.

'McLean called it,' he said. 'McLean called it from space and it answered. But it couldn't penetrate directly to the ground. There's a man in that satellite.'

It was Sheila who responded first. 'It could be any one of a dozen countries who've put that satellite up,' she said. 'There could be many reasons why they haven't made it public. But it was somewhere that the alien force could reach directly? Take over and use to project its power down to earth? And from that it could in the same way control McLean.'

Maxwell thought again of McLean and his fate, and wondered what would be found in the satellite in the wake of the departing alien force.

Sammy's eye caught Duncan's world map. Rising, he took a felt pen and completed the join-up of the lines. There, stark, was a pentagram.

'Coincidence,' said Sammy, returning to his chair. A new power was loose in the world, Maxwell realised, and old symbols like pentagrams were no longer relevant.

'This force,' Livingstone asked carefully, 'where is it now? What is it doing?'

But Sammy was fast asleep.

'I can tell you,' Elaine Bateman said. 'We now control the force and we are sending it out to the Trojan position at Jupiter. What we have to do now is to find a way of communicating with it, so that it can be beneficial to humanity, maybe as a means of exerting condign power.'

She let the words hang. Somehow, she was no longer an ordinary woman. Now she had authority. Now she had power, and it showed.

Maxwell felt a new chill of unease. Condign power. To root out evil. To punish. But where might it end? Authoritarian rule by a small group of all-powerful people who need never *meet* each other, need never make pronouncements, but simply act as they saw fit.

Sheila had reacted to the mention of the Trojan position. 'It's like a natural holding area,' she said. 'There are asteroids trapped there now. The distance from Earth doesn't vary much, proportionately, during the year, and it would take only minor perturbations to keep it in view – even on the far side of the sun from us.'

Maxwell made one last appeal. 'Why don't you let it go, send it towards the stars?'

Elaine Bateman shook her head, as if she were dealing with a none-too-bright child.

'We don't want to do that.'

IN THE WEEKS that followed, life returned more or less to normal at the institute, as the winter research programme got into its stride. To most of the staff it seemed that Maxwell was generally pleased about the current progress. Only Duncan – along with Jason Brown at the Computing Centre – shared his preoccupation with national and international news, gathering a stream of cuttings and setting them out in various patterns.

The first obviously untrivial one was when the Chinese government announced the failure of a secret man-in-space programme. The occupant of the spacecraft had been testing a metabolism-slowing drug for long space voyages, but had not been revived when the appropriate command from the ground was transmitted. Nor had the controllers been able to bring the spacecraft back.

Immediately, as a humanitarian gesture, the United States government proposed a rescue. For once, Maxwell found himself hoping that a gesture of international goodwill would founder in some diplomatic nicety, but the plans went ahead all too smoothly, and the drama was played out in live broadcasts on the TV screens of the world.

Maxwell watched as two astronauts crossed by Orbital Transfer Vehicle from the US Space Station. As they entered the Chinese spacecraft, both reported a mental shock as the last tendrils of the force leaped through their minds and fled towards the orbit of Jupiter

They had expected to find the Chinese astronaut in a coma, but he was dead, only the head preserved; and with the last of the force removed, that too was decaying before their eyes.

Cutting off the grisly description, the commentators emphasised the iron self-control the astronauts were showing. Maxwell, watching, wondered if all that control was the result of rigid training, or whether it was already coming from another source. He thought of the powerful web reaching out from the earth to the orbit of Jupiter, with humanity gradually being enfolded into its invisible but all-powerful strands. *Captured by the incredible, which is the very essence of dreams.*

My favourite moment in the previous story is the emergence of the pentagram, although by then its usefulness is over. In The Square Fella, *too, the big moment is the revelation of a shape. I have to thank Pete Clements for his help in the 'What if....?' game which led to this story. For the title, I have to thank Drew Moyes and apologise to the shade of Brendan Behan.*

Duncan Lunan
THE SQUARE FELLA

'THE DUKE HAS WITHDRAWN HIS SUPPORT FOR YOUR project.'

The visitor was having difficulty with the thin air at this altitude, having flown straight up from the coast with no time for acclimatisation. In the briefing room, he was outnumbered by Leon, Michael, Gordon and Beatrice; but if either factor reduced his assurance, he did not allow it to show. 'You are to suspend operations at once, and return with me to the city.'

'Out of the question!' Leon snapped. 'We are in the final stages of preparation. I could argue that it would be more dangerous now to dismantle the rocket than to launch. *Certainly* it would be more dangerous to leave it upright. That vehicle out there is the most powerful ever assembled by man!'

'Just the point, sir,' said the Duke's envoy. 'His Highness's neighbours have grown concerned. From this high ground, your vehicle could deliver a ton or more of explosives or incendiaries to any city around the central sea. You and the Duke must prove that your intention is purely scientific, before you may proceed.'

'The point is absurd,' said Michael. 'I speak as calculator of the trajectory. To reach any lowland point from there, the rocket would have to rise thousands of miles, as indeed it is intended to do. But the same could be achieved with a smaller vehicle from anywhere downslope, and with more accuracy.'

'I am not an expert in these matters,' said the envoy, brushing the objection aside. 'They will be for the Church to decide, when the objectors' petitions are heard.'

'As I thought,' said Leon. 'The Church is the principal objector, is it not?'

'Your ideas are well known to be controversial. Personally, I take no interest in academic disputes …'

'And yet you are here to intervene in one, and in the most drastic fashion! Let me show you what is at stake.' Leon crossed to the first of the charts on the wall. 'Here is our world, as we perceive it: a great bowl, with the life-giving sea at its centre. As we travel away from the sea, the slope grows ever steeper and the air more thin – as you notice.' The visitor had subsided into a chair and was visibly short of breath. 'We are only twenty-five miles upslope. Ten miles from here, you could not remain conscious without breathing apparatus. Seven hundred and fifty miles up, we now know, the atmosphere becomes negligible and there is no vestige of life. By long tradition, the four great mountains on the ridges above us are the corners by which the Gods hold up the world, like a great sheet.

'If they released their hold, the sheet would flatten, the air and water spread out, and life would be extinguished. But can we believe that — how can we believe it — when we learn that the ridges are four thousand miles above us; the mountains seventeen hundred and fifty miles higher still; so that most of the Bowl is barren and lifeless.'

'What alternative is there? Are you an atheist, sir, do you argue that the existence of life in these favoured conditions is an accident?'

'No, no, that's too absurd to consider. But what we must consider is that the world is not shaped as we see it. Are you familiar with the results of Colom's expedition?'

'A vast effort, which the Queen herself had to finance, at great cost and to no purpose. A madman, driven by some supposed insight about a world beyond the Bowl, travelled thousands of miles through airless waste. He failed to reach the ridge, and only that saved him from plunging off into the infinity beyond.'

'That's the official version,' said Leon. 'What wasn't given out, and very few of us know, is that when the slope grew too steep near the top, Colom left the vehicle and went up alone, with breathing apparatus. He reached the ridge, stood upon it, and saw what lay beyond.'

'And that was?' Not even this visitor could refrain from asking, though he feigned indifference.

'Another Bowl – from that high viewpoint, indistinguishable from our own. A descending slope, at right-angles to the one he had climbed, and extending equally far below him.'

'Probably it *was* our own. Your madman was too far gone from weakness and lack of air to tell the difference, I suppose.'

'I have another suggestion,' said Leon, turning to the next diagram. 'Ever since we've had aircraft – and with everyone living on a slope, *that* was inevitable – men have been trying to use them for warfare, to drop things from them and shoot things at them. We wouldn't have rockets otherwise. But once projective theory was perfected – for which we have Michael here to thank – it was discovered that the centre of attraction in our world lies four thousand miles below the centre of the Bowl.'

'And so?'

'And so that allows a much vaster world than we supposed. If the North ridge has another Bowl beyond it, the same must be true of the other ridges – and the far ridges of those Bowls – and so on, around the surface of a spheroid. Each Bowl could have its own air, ocean and life … even intelligent life, though completely isolated from our own.'

'And each with its own Gods, at its corners, living on those airless plateaux you've drawn between the mountains? I see now why you have to be stopped. Even the speculation is dangerous, and I shall report as much. In giving foundations to the Bowl, you remove support from the faith! For the record, how many worlds and Gods do you postulate?'

'Thirty-six Bowls, at the least, though one must be smaller than our own. As for Gods, who can say?'

'You have already said quite enough!' A fit of coughing

racked the envoy, as he rose to his feet. 'By the authority of the Church and the Duke, I order you to cease all preparations, and dismantle what is in hand ...'

'No,' said Leon. The sheer effrontery of it took the envoy's breath away, and in this high place, he would have trouble regaining it. As he collapsed, coughing violently, he managed to gasp. 'The troops will stop you ...'

'As I thought,' said Michael, pushing the others towards the door. 'Those rumours of manoeuvres in the highlands were just too convenient. Leon, we must launch at once. Gordon, are you ready?'

'You can't just leave that man in there – ' Beatrice protested. But the two philosophers had already gone, one to the control room and the other towards the rocket.

'He's less danger to us immobilised in there.' Gordon told her. 'No doubt someone will get him an air cylinder ... I have to get ready for the flight. And I have to make sure Leon and Michael get you out of here, on one of the aircraft, before the troops arrive.' Beatrice was the only woman here, as a special privilege to himself, and he didn't want her to fall into the the hands of the Duke's enemies.

'We should have had more time!' They had followed Leon, more slowly, towards the rocket which now towered ahead of them. 'Gordon, it's so dangerous. Is it worth it, just to learn the shape of the world?'

'It's time to find out – it's as simple as that. Don't worry, I'll come back.' He kissed her in the midst of the activity Leon had galvanised, and left her to climb the gantry which would soon be wheeled away.

'Let's go over it once again,' said Leon, as Gordon settled himself in the couch. 'Your launch will be vertical, all the way. Peak altitude will be sixty thousand miles, fifteen world radii, flight time will be twenty-four hours. Centripetal attraction will be enough to make sure you come down in air. You'll be high enough at peak to see clearly into the surrounding Bowls. And if that other crazy idea is correct, and the world rotates under you,

you'll travel in effect along a great circle, over ten of the Bowls in all, and land at a symmetrical point on the far side of our own – in which case Colom's crew will pick you up. Better hope that's true, if there are troops on the way here,' he added, brusquely, and clasped Gordon's hand before banging shut the hatch.

Now there was time to think about it, in the long pause before the launch. Time to think about the failure of the previous test, the attempt to put a reflecting sphere like an artificial sun into orbit around the world. The trajectory had been good, according to observers upslope, but the speck had never reappeared over the rim of the world, though the observers remained on station until lack of air forced them down. Hence the plan, this time, to go straight up and remain in view throughout – unless of course the world really did rotate with respect to the stars and the sun …

How could appearances be so deceptive? Impressed as he was by Colom's account, if only in defiance of the clerical critics, what kind of Gods could create so misleading a world? The team had discussed this only the previous night, over a bottle of wine, thinking they still had days to prepare for the mission. Had they all met before, Leon had speculated, in another Bowl or even another world, and argued over its shape – perhaps a very different shape from this? Michael had pointed out the regularities of the world: the stars, for instance, evenly spaced and giving just enough warmth to keep the Bowl from freezing at night. 'Perhaps it's not a true cosmos – just a bubble, or a box. A great All-Fool's joke by the Gods, or beings less than gods.'

The lowlands were abuzz with the issue, from the coastal cities to the highest towns on the periphery. The argument wasn't just between science and the church: the patrons of the rocket and crawler programmes had their own rivalries, and duels had been fought over the merits of two approaches which should have been complementary. Only the faithful could accept that the issue shouldn't be settled by experiment, and the supposed military threat of Leon's rocket was pure invention. Anyone who believed that would believe that the grazing herds up here had longer legs on one side that the other, to run at high speed around the slope of the Bowl.

These were stupendous days, Gordon and Beatrice had agreed, as they had watched the descending sun reflected on the burnished flank of the rocket. When it was gone, the glare of the work lights had almost obliterated the even spread of stars glowing above them. 'If faith rests on a lie,' they had pledged later, 'let faith fall!' The challenge and the daring of their response made it seem as if nothing could stop them; but the envoy from downslope had returned them to reality. It had taken all the power of Colom's patrons, including the Queen, to keep him out of prison or the insane isylum. If troops overran the launch site, destroying the rocket or arresting the scientists, Leon's patron could do little about it. It was not an issue over which to go to war.

Outside, the aircraft had taken off to sweep the surrounding slope before the launch. Gordon had insisted Beatrice be in one, to escape if there were soldiers closing in. And sure enough, one of the aircraft was back already, warning lights flashing to the periscopes of the armoured control room.

If only they could exchange spoken messages! Some of the experimenters in the Duke's laboratories believed they could make it possible, across the central sea or even to the heights Gordon would reach today. Objectors had wanted the mission postponed until that would be possible. But as he had told Beatrice, it was time to find the answer *now*. As if to confirm it, a red flare soared from the blockhouse, and beneath him brilliant flame cracked into being at the base of the rocket. The Launch Master gave the solid-fuel thrust a moment to stabilise before releasing the clamps, and then he was away, watching the shadow of the rocket and the smoke trail racing the vehicle itself up-slope. His fate would be governed by the gyroscopes in Leon's steering system: he had no control, and in any case the acceleration held him immobile as expected.

Going up vertically, with reference to gravity, he was out of the air much faster than he would have been climbing or flying up the slope. There was a little buffeting at first, but that soon faded away. Already the grasslands were thinning out, well away to port; patterns of moss and lichen, with no snow at this time of year, merged into bare rock. He was out of the atmosphere: he saw sunlight flash on the lens of one of Leon's high-altitude trackers. The heliograph messages had alerted at least one team in time for them to cover the early launch.

The first stage burned out, plunging him into the weightlessness he had sometimes generated in soaring aircraft. He counted off the seconds, one, two, three, *four,* and the second stage fired and disconnected. A brief oscillation, caught by the gyros and the vanes, and up, up he went, the jet roaring closer behind him now, while outside the sky turned black and the stars came out, as he had seen them in sunlight when training up-slope. The acceleration wasn't unbearable; higher than in the water-driven centrifuge, but more purposeful, with the knowledge that he was actually going somewhere. The gyros showed no deviation from the vertical climb, the graphite vanes in the exhaust had not been needed. The face of the Bowl, off to port, was a racing blur of light and shadow, still constantly receding. Only the failed satellite had gone higher than this.

The capsule tumbled as the charge sputtered out and expelled him, but the cold gas jets let him stabilise it. With the heat shield pointed towards the sun, and the Bowl inverted 'above' him, he seemed to be falling out of it into space. But in fact he was slowing constantly, as the central mass pulled him back. The entry shield was facing the sun, out of sight below, so it shouldn't be necessary to rotate the capsule to cool it. There was a periscope arrangement with a revolving mirror, so that he could continue observations even if spinning proved necessary, but it would limit his field of view. For the moment, the shield seemed to be coping.

He was amazed at how much he could see from this altitude. For a while, even without the telescope the patterns of cultivated land were clear in the lowland plains. The overall circulation of the clouds was clearly displayed, and below them he could see concentric rings of colour in the central sea. He was noting down all observations, just in case he shouldn't be alive when the capsule returned to the Bowl, though of all possibilities that seemed the least likely, when life-support systems had been so thoroughly developed in the slope crawler programme. The cost had been high, recorded in the notebooks of failed expeditions – the notebooks of men who would walk away from a failed crawler, to give their companions more time to wait for rescue. If his own life was to be forfeited, well, others had gone that way before. Better to die seeking answers than at the hands of the Church which forbade the questions.

Within an hour, he had confirmed the less likely hypothesis under test. The Bowl *was* rotating, leaving him behind as he rose out of it; his vertical climb was taking on the elliptic contour of a ballistic trajectory. The observers below would see him moving westward among the stars, falling behind the creeping sun, if they still had him. Inevitably, now, he must go over the rim of the world like the failed satellite, and he had only Michael's word that inevitably he must return. If the world was not symmetrical, he was doomed – but there was more exhilaration in it than fear.

By the second hour, however, the spheroidal hypothesis was in trouble. He should by now have been over the western edge of the Bowl, had Leon been right, but instead he had still to pass over the central sea. If he had been deflected back towards the east ridge from the vertical during the second-stage burn, he would now be crossing the Bowl too slowly, higher than he should be, and would come down in some other bowl on the great circle or on one of the airless plateaux between them. That at least would be a quick death, since only air could slow the capsule down. In another Bowl, there might be a higher civilisation which could help him get home …

But the gyros had been true, according to the instruments. If so, the geometry of the world had to be quite different from Leon's prediction. Since the Bowl turned under sun and stars, and the central mass lay far below it, was there a counterweight beyond that? He would be at his furthest from the centre when he passed it; but if was less massive and further from the centre than the Bowl, collision might be inevitable. It would explain the disappearance of the satellite. What an extraordinary way to die, smeared flat like an insect, amid the ruins of drawings no-one would ever see.

The known world had shrunk to a misty, distorted patch in the centre of the rocky expanse of the Bowl. The face below him swept evenly round to encompass it, the effect of its concavity much less than he had expected. Perhaps his eyes were over-compensating for the lack of atmospheric refraction. The sun had passed over the western edge, still drawing ahead of him, and was illuminating whatever lay beyond. Soon Gordon, too, would be able to see over the approaching ridge. He forced himself to down some food, and waited in suspense as the world turned slowly below.

He could see over the ridge now, and there was another slope beyond. Far beyond, there lay another ridge, broken in places by steep slides of rock. There was a world outside the Bowl, and it was another Bowl, edged with ridges and mountains of its own —

But with straight edges. There were no high-altitude, airless plateaux, inhabited by Gods or otherwise. The two 'Bowls' met at the West ridge, all the way along, and now that he was over it he could see that the ridge itself was a straight line. The new 'Bowl's' inner face dropped steeply away from it, at an exact right-angle to the old, and from this height neither face showed any concavity whatever. At last he could dismiss the distortions of perspective, compensate for the vastness of the view, and recognise what he truly saw. The shock was overwhelming.

"The World is a cube!" Gordon wrote on his pad, and he underlined till he couldn't draw for laughing and the capsule was rocking. The wildest theorist patronised by the Duke would never have dreamed of it. All down the ages the priests had likened the Bowl to a great square of cloth, held up by the Gods at its four corners to keep the air and water in the centre. And behold, gravity alone was responsible, the square had been flat all along – not just flat, not just a square, but the face of a *cube!* Laughter threatened to overwhelm him again. He could see, now, that the second face had its own central pool of air and water – and perhaps living beings, fooled by their Gods into thinking they lived in a Bowl which was the whole of Creation.

To his trained eye, it was obvious that it had been created. In vacuum the mountains were very bright, like cut gems. *Cut gems, deliberately shaped.* Though half-obscured by rock slides, there were faint lines of stress emanating from them, diagonals and intersecting curves, as if space itself was distorted to hold the world in shape. Surely only Gods could make a world, much less keep it in a shape which was against its raw nature. Could it all just be to create niches for life, as if for study? The true purpose was unfathomable.

Somehow he must get back to reveal this, whatever the personal cost. He had been sketching assiduously; they wouldn't put this down to lack of oxygen, or heat exhaustion. But was return possible? Obviously the Gods' web of forces must affect his trajectory, and if he got outside it, he might never come down but drift forever amid the lattice of stars.

The face below held a world larger than his own, so the air must be thicker. Certainly the clouds were higher and more extensive, giving only glimpses of the surface below. The central sea was much bigger down there, and temperatures were obviously higher. He saw no sign of intelligence, though from this height, that proved little. If there was life down there on the second face, it might be quite unlike his own; the two 'Bowls' were as completely isolated as if they sat on different worlds. The towering barrier of the ridge had to be overcome for any kind of contact, and only intelligent life could make that effort. No birds, insects or winds crossed the ridge to seed one place with the life of the other, and thousands of miles of rock separated them underground. Would it be possible to make a tunnel through? A vehicle could 'fall' through it, slowing after the midpoint. Beyond doubt, knowing that other 'Bowls' existed, men like Leon and Colom would want to visit them.

His own Bowl was lost to view. On the assumption that he would have stayed over it, he had been scheduled to sleep for six hours during the flight; and as he gained height and the view became less detailed, he allowed sleep to take him. When he awoke, he was over the third face of the cube, and beginning to descend. Michael's predictions might yet bring him home, though certainly not where troops directed by the Church would be expecting him. What else, he wondered, was happening behind him meantime? Had Beatrice made good her escape, and were Leon and Michael now facing the wrath of the Church? Or had they tracked the capsule, guessing wrongly from his slow movement west, and given him up for lost? Even so, some members of the team would be envying him what he must he seeing now, impossible though it would be for them to imagine: from this height, he could see the world plainly as a cube.

The third face was much different at the centre, with thin air, no sea, and hardly any clouds. Markings under the cap of atmosphere suggested there might once have been a sea, but if so the water had long since escaped. Bands of red and ochre stained the ground, as though the surface had oxidised. Gordon could see no clear signs of life, though some circular forms might be the work of intelligence; like the traces of some colossal bombardment.

The capsule was well on its way down, beginning to overtake the sun as it gained speed on the descending leg of its trajectory. By now Gordon was sure the trajectory itself was correct: he would come down at sunrise on the western edge of the known Bowl. He would be glad to have the sun back under the shield, meantime – he had had to spin the capsule several times to cool it, using up precious gas, and the glare was an annoyance.

The fourth face, as he crossed it, was another extreme: a turbulent, opaque atmosphere, streaked with colours and some-times lit from below by the flashes of violent storms.

Were these the laboratories where the Gods tried out their ideas, on the formation of life and its evolution? It had been suggested, though with great caution, that life in his own Bowl had not always been as it was today: it was a matter on which the Church had yet to rule. The differing conditions on the four faces might represent different stages in the evolution of life, or perhaps evolution in different conditions. The polar faces must be dead, in permanent shadow except where ridges caught the sun, unless the warmth from the stars was enough to keep the air gaseous and sustain something strange in the twilight.

His mission should be repeated in darkness, to look for city lights on the other faces …

Well ahead of the sun, Gordon passed over the last ridge into his own 'Bowl', a vast black field cutting off the stars. He was right on schedule: the trackers should pick him up easily, since he was in full sunlight. As he hurtled on, he had to hope for the last required accuracy: it would be tragic to miss the atmosphere and end the mission by crashing on to bare rock. As he turned the capsule for the final descent, above him he saw a great cascade of light down the ridges as the Sun broke over the edge of the Bowl.

He had set the vehicle spinning, and a fiery glow built built up around it as he plunged towards the western slope. This, he realised, was the Gods last chance: he was coming back with the shape of the world, the plurality of worlds, and doubts of the Gods' godhood. It was the last chance to burn him with his knowledge.

The chance was missed. The fire died away, the capsule's fins were extended to stop the spin. The parachutes opened and the falling craft steadied in the sky, over the forests of the west highlands. Down there, Colom would be organising aircraft and ground parties to search for him. They must plan how to spread the new knowledge: slowly, by secret organisation, or shouted from the housetops at risk of martyrdom?

He hoped there would be time to decide. One way or another, his knowledge *must* be spread. His mind lingered on that as the capsule descended into the trees, marching like an army down the long slope of the land.

As well as being Professor of Astronomy at Glasgow University and a well-known psychic researcher, Archie Roy is the author of thrillers such as Deadlight *(John Long, 1968) with SF and supernatural themes; these have recently been reissued under his own imprint, Apogee Books. In* Sable Night *(1973) we first met the researchers Meredith and Bourne, and their antipathy to each other continued in* The Devil in the Darkness *(1978). In Chapter 13 of that book, they have the argument which leads to this new story. Here we find them in a world subtly different from ours, a world in which Glasgow University didn't move from the High Street to Gilmorehill in 1870, and in which William Kingdon Clifford anticipated the theories we attribute to Einstein.*

In this final story of the collection, Archie will bring us back to reality in due course. Fasten your seat-belts, though, because it will be a bumpy ride.

Archie Roy
KING OF ENGLAND I WILL DIE!

MEREDITH WALKED UP THE WINDING HIGH STREET, the late afternoon sunshine warm on his shoulders, taking in the facades of the old Glasgow buildings. As always, he travelled light, his only encumbrance a soft brown leather valise containing a change of clothes, a scratchpad and a favourite book or two. Among them was his old paperback copy of *Richard III*. In truth he knew so much of it by heart that he hardly needed to carry it about with him, but somehow he regarded this particular copy as an old friend. His early schooling had been surprisingly meagre for a man of his present position as Regius Professor of Mediaeval History at the University of York. But he still remembered vividly the day he had found the secondhand copy in the book barrow in the Shambles. He'd never understood why he'd bought it – for sixpence – after browsing through it but he'd done so and somehow Richard's words and character – as portrayed by Shakespeare – had sparked something in his own make-up. The cripple-king battling and scheming against his enemies resonated with some hitherto slumbering force within him, propelling him to night classes, examinations, university and up the seemingly infinitely tall academic ladder until he achieved his present position and international reputation.

> *Now is the winter of our discontent*
> *Made glorious summer by this sun of York;*
> *And all the clouds that lour'd upon our house*
> *In the deep bosom of the ocean buried.*

Yes. The King had been a good friend to him. He grinned, gripped the rough handle of the valise and marched on up the street, noting the spire of the Cathedral rising into view above the steep roofs.

The train from York had been on time: part of the journey had been spent chewing over Bourne's unexpected invitation. Finally he had given up his profitless speculation. The only thing he could be sure of was that dear old Bourne in some way hoped to do him down. Possibly he'd have been wiser to refuse the invitation, to plead a previous engagement. But no. He'd taken the bait and now was here, his mouth quirked, 'like a lamb to the slaughter'? Well, he'd soon see. At one state in his speculation on the gently-rocking train, annoyed at the futile thoughts squirreling round his brain, he'd picked up a couple of tabloids a passenger had discarded when he'd left the train at Settle. As Meredith idly flipped over the pages he marvelled afresh at the frenetic sensationalism, the total contempt for the intelligence of the readers. Without any regard for truth each concocted an endless purvey of spicy garish headlines screaming for attention – *Chambermaid Gives Birth to a Crocodile – Submarine Finds Lost Atlantis – Ancient Greece Was a Martian Colony – House of Lords Gang-Raped Debbie in Non-Stop Orgy*. Apart from pandering to the prurient curiosity inherent in most human beings, their tendency to slight paranoic suspicion was also catered for. The *Daily Sun* revealed that the unprecedented and growing numbers of disappearances of people in all walks of life, the alarmingly increasing number of madmen reported, the multi-death bomb explosions and inexplicable breakdown of dams, machinery and communications on a world-wide scale were the result of an all-out assault on civilisation by a consortium of international terrorist organisations with agents slotted into all levels of society from postman to Pope, from policeman to President. Not to be outdone, the *Mirror* revealed that these events were a new attempt by aliens to destabilise Earth prior to an all-out invasion. After tossing the paper aside, Meredith had contented himself on the run up to Carlise with the view from the carriage window of peaceful rolling hills and dales drifting past.

At the porter's box in the Old College entrance, Meredith confirmed the advice Bourne had sent him regarding the location of the Department of History. It was housed in one of the newer brick buildings built during the last expansion of higher education, a functional streamlined block that jarred in its concrete contrast to the older neighbouring dark-stoned crow-step Scottish architecture. As he crossed the worn quadrangle flagstones he tried to recall what had stood in its place. It was ten years since he'd last been in Glasgow to give a seminar. Oh yes. Some of the old Professors' Square had gone.

He climbed the stairs, found Bourne's office and entered. At a desk in the outer office a woman secretary, fair-haired, middle-aged, looked up.

'Richard Meredith to see Professor Bourne. He's expecting me.'

A minute later he was seated in a brown leather armchair before Bourne's desk. Behind it, Bourne, his thin intelligent, supercilious face professing pleasure, welcomed him. Meredith noted with amusement that Bourne's chair was higher than his.

'My dear chap, so good of you to come. Know how busy you must be. You've been back from the Granada visit only a few days. I know how it is. You find a mountain of things to do piled up on your desk … '

Meredith let him prattle on, enjoying the air conditioning after his walk up the High Street, contenting himself with trying to gauge what kind of pit Bourne had dug for him. They had crossed swords many times in journals, at conferences, on committees. Each knew the other to be more than capable, and it certainly was not unheard of in science and the arts for two first rate researchers to oppose each other's research findings, but it was much more than that. Their personalities were such that they fundamentally clashed. Meredith knew that Bourne regarded him as a jumped-up peasant who had got the Chair Bourne had been entitled to. When they were both scheduled to speak in London at a meeting of the Royal Society of History, the attendance would be invariably larger than usual because of the expected verbal fireworks. And we never fail to perform, he thought ruefully.

'Now before we do anything else, Meredith, let me take you across the Square to the Annexe. You'll doubtless want to unpack – ' his pale-blue eyes flickered with irony at Meredith's battered valise ' – and freshen up before dinner.' He rose. 'You'll find the Annexe comfortable. You have bedroom, private sitting-room and the use of the breakfast room. Converted from one of the former Professor's houses. A bit old-fashioned but very comfortable. And you have of course temporary membership of the College Club while you're here …'

He kept up a flow of social chit-chat – almost as a smokescreen, Meredith thought – until he left Meredith alone in the second-storey bedroom.

As he shaved after his bath, Meredith regarded his image in the steamy bathroom mirror and reflected that so far Bourne had revealed nothing. At times though, his mask of solicitous friendship had slipped to show a momentary crowing 'I know something you don't' face. Meredith grimaced at his reflection.

Cannot a plain man live and think no harm,
But thus his simple truth must be abus'd
By silken, sly, insinuating Jacks?

At dinner in the College Club the situation somewhat clarified. Apart from Bourne and Meredith, there were three others present at the polished oak table, under one of the big leaded stained-glass windows still ablaze with the evening sunshine. Peter Maitland, a thin, worried man prematurely bald, turned out to be a specialist in nineteenth-century history. He seemed to hold Bourne in high esteem. John Palmer, dark-haired, quiet and watchful, was harder to place. The only woman present, whose interesting face just failed to be beautiful, seemed friendly enough, content to enjoy the food and conversation. Bourne introduced her as Doctor Jane Salisbury but did not define what she was a doctor of.

By the time the port and nuts stage had been reached, Meredith's capital of patience had almost gone into overdraft. Bourne had been in sparkling mood, in the role of gracious host, drawing Meredith out on some of the two men's past disagreements without, Meredith thought suspiciously, any of his usual bitchiness when Meredith scored a point. Occasionally Bourne, as if the other guests knew nothing about Meredith, would enlighten them regarding as escapade in his career though the latter was pretty sure the others had already been well briefed.

'As Peter's well aware, Professor Meredith and I take up opposing stances on the two basic theories of history. For myself, I see no reason to believe that the course of history would change beyond a few details if the vast majority of individuals had had different lives or indeed had not been born. The great shapers of history are agriculture, communication, science, technology, religion, commerce, hunger, climatic changes. Certainly forceful individuals appear in history and act as catalysts or as tiny crystals triggering off a wave of crystallisation when society becomes a supersaturated solution, but the correct circumstances must be present. Whether Caesar died in 44 BC or happened to escape the conspirators' daggers, the Roman Empire would still have evolved and decayed, the life-styles of most of its population would have shown no essential differences. If King Harold had not been killed by Duke William in 1066 because William did not exist, the times were such that England would still have been successfully invaded sooner or later from France.' He raised his head to glance at Meredith even as he refilled his glass. Meredith thought the ruby glint of the port resembled the spark of anger he felt. Bourne continued to expound his thesis.

'Even in science it's likely that the great discoveries and inventions would have appeared at the right times, so often have such achievements been made almost simultaneously by two or even three people working independently of each other. Calculus, radio, television, aircraft. I forget who it was who said: "there's nothing so powerful as an idea whose time has come." Bourne smiled. 'Meredith, on the other hand, … supports the individual viewpoint of history. The whole course of history would change if a fishwife in Arbroath on a particular day happened to sell just one more herring.'

John Palmer forestalled Meredith's retort.

'Nonsense, Bourne. I'm sure Dr. Meredith thinks no such thing. There must be innumerable everyday actions by countless people that leave the lives of the population completely un-modified. In the Middle Ages people in remote villages or on island settlements could live their lives largely uninfluenced by important events.'

Meredith nodded. 'Agreed. But on the other hand many people in history, even totally humble, *obscure* people, have been in a situation where a simple action or decision of theirs if reversed or cancelled or even modified, would change the future. I once discussed this with my mathematical colleagues. They talked of the flow of history as a solution of a set of highly nonlinear differential equations, one variable for each human being, with other parameters present to represent those great natural history shapers you talked of, Bourne.' He smirked blandly. Meredith continued. 'They also said the flow of solu-tions of these equations would be – what did they call it? – yes, hyper-unstable and chaotic beyond imagining. In other words even tiny changes at a given time in the values of the variables and parameter might – no, probably would – produce vast chan-ges in the subsequent directions of the flow of solutions. He glanced round the table and shrugged. 'It made sense to me.'

Jane Salisbury addressed him, abruptly changing the

topic of conversation though Meredith warned himself that it was highly probable nothing introduced at this dinner-table was unrehearsed. God, he thought, how paranoic can you get? Nonetheless he paid careful attention to the woman's words.

'Are you one of those historians who attach weight to accounts of ostensible former lives as an aid to historical research?'

Meredith frowned. Over the years he had read with some interest reports published by hypnotherapists of their hypnotised subjects being regressed to eras long before their birth and describing, as if they were experiencing them, the events of a former life. The accounts were vivid, full of detail, and usually consistent in that the subject invariably, hypnotised again after many years and taken back to the same era, would describe the same life again, same incidents, same family, same friends and acquaintances. Meredith had remained sceptical about the reality of such 'lives'. Although some of them were extremely plausible with details consistent with known historical facts, or social conditions of that era, they could be taken to be role-playing by the subject to please the hypnotist. The bones of the dramatisation would be clothed with the flesh of those innumerable snippets of fact culled from a lifetime's casual reading, or listening or looking at pictures, only a tiny percentage of which the conscious mind could normally recall. Or perhaps, he had thought, much of the material was actually snatched by paranormal means – telepathy or clairvoyance – from living people's minds or from the books and other sources possessing such data. He had been intrigued but somehow had not felt that the strange phenomenon would be of much value in the solution of any of history's mysteries hidden, as the Irishman put it, within the mists of iniquity. But he knew that some of the younger historians had toyed with the idea even, he remembered, creating a Journal of Psychohistory. And with a feeling of unease, he also recalled that Bourne had pontificated on television about hidebound reactionaries who thought that genuine historical research should confine itself to the reading of dusty rent-rolls, mediaeval chronicles and Parliamentary parchments. Surely Bourne did not take such things as regression hypnosis seriously? But yet he might. It was precisely the kind of 'progressive' approach he might feel would add to his reputation as a sharp open-minded up-to-the-minute historian. For it was the sort of thrilling dramatic type of thing that appealed to the public and made good television.

He saw that Jane Salisbury awaited his reply and described briefly his reservations. She nodded.

'I can understand your worries. How can we be sure the subject is not role-playing in one way or another. It does seem, at first glance to be a "heads I win, tails you lose" situation. If you can check the details of the ostensible former life, then how can you be really sure the subject had not at some time picked up such data and has merely forgotten it? One the other hand if you can't check it, how do you know you are dealing with a real former life?' She smiled. 'Of course it's not as simple as that. If you know the subject's life-history pretty exhaustively and he had been – let's say – a practically illiterate shepherd all his days and he comes up with a rich former life which in checking requires a long difficult search in obscure archival material scattered widely, then you're going to find it difficult – to put it mildly – to explain away such a life as simple role-playing. And suppose you got a case where the subject reveals that he or she during former life buried something valuable or hid jewels in a secret room in a country house and you went and found them. What then?' Her smile became an almost impish grin, transforming her former almost dour expression.

Meredith nodded slowly, intrigued in spite of himself.

'Clairvoyance?'

'Oh come now, Meredith,' Bourne was gently scathing in his manner. 'That's just a name given to a process no respectable scientist believes exists.' He glanced round the table. 'No. If you took the trouble to examine what's being done these days in psychohistory you'd see that there's a great deal of hard evidence that at least some ostensible former lives are genuine.'

'You take it seriously?'

'Indeed we do. And have been doing so for the past year.' He watched the expression of Meredith's face. 'Oh, I must admit I was sceptical at first but this past year has changed all that. Dr Salisbury had changed my attitude entirely.'

Meredith thought: he's not usually so eager to give praise to anyone else. Then he saw the way Bourne looked at Jane Salisbury and understood. As far as Bourne was capable of it, he'd fallen for the Salisbury woman. God, he thought, I wonder if she knows what she's let herself in for. Maybe I'd better listen very carefully for I'm sure all this is not by accident. His suspicion strengthened when Bourne rose and suggested they adjourn to his office. 'We have privacy there and I feel certain, my dear Meredith, that you'll be intrigued at that we have to show you.'

They crossed the lamp-lit quadrangle and climbed the turret stairs to Bourne's spacious office. Once inside John Palmer sat down on the large cushioned couch. Peter Maitland, over by the curtained window, set up a recorder on a small table, and busied himself with it while Bourne took his seat behind the desk. Jane Salisbury sat down beside John Palmer. Obviously they were all waiting for Bourne to explain what was scheduled. Meredith's watchfulness increased.

God keep me from false friends! he thought and listened expectantly.

'What we're about to show you arose from a research programme by Jane and her colleagues in the Psychology Department into ostensible former lives under hypnotism. I learned that over many months they had collected hundreds of former lives from as many subjects – most of them being students.' He grinned. 'One of the rare fringe benefits of doing research in a university is an almost inexhaustible supply of "guinea pigs". Of course not all the subjects were students. Some were outsiders or members of staff.

'Anyway there were so many that even after you divided the ostensible former lives up by century and country you had quite a number in each category. And so you could do a sort of statistical analysis of the lives in a category, comparing the various details of clothes, food, social customs, houses, agriculture, professions and so on for consistency. And of course we found, as expected, that the overwhelming majority of past lives were completely obscure, boring and in fact often "nasty, brutish and short".'

So far, Meredith thought, though interesting it was not the sort of research breakthrough that a man would parade before his deadly rival. There had to be more to it than that.

'No famous former lives? No Cleopatras, Julius Caesars? No Roger Bacons, no Shakespeares?'

'There were a few, a very few, but palpably false.' Bourne turned to look at John Palmer. 'John, however, came up with something rather intriguing. He became interested in our research and volunteered to be hypnotised. He produced one former life. Not famous directly, but in an oblique way by no means unimportant. But let him speak for himself. All right, John?'

Palmer nodded. He relaxed into a corner of the couch, his hands clasped in his lap. Jane Salisbury turned towards him. In a quite, firm voice she said: 'John, you will now enter the hypnotic state. Go to sleep, John.'

His eyes closed, his body seemed to relax still further. Jane nodded to Bourne.

'He's in.'

Meredith blinked. 'As easy as that?'

'Yes. He's been conditioned to that particular sentence in past sessions.'

'But how do you know he's really under and –' Meredith hesitated, 'not faking it?'

Bourne grinned. Jane rose, crossed to Bourne's desk and took a pencil from a green coffee mug bristling with an armoury of pens and pencils. She sat down on the couch again and glanced at Meredith.

'Watch!' She touched Palmer's left hand. 'I'm going to touch you there with a red-hot iron. You will feel no pain but the next touch is with the red-hot iron. Now.'

She pushed the end of the pencil against the back of Palmer's hand, held it there for a few seconds then withdrew it. To Meredith's astonishment, over the next minute an ugly serum-filled blister, a nimbus of angry inflamed flesh surrounding it, appeared. Palmer's face remained peaceful and detached. With soothing counter-suggestions, the woman then reversed the process. Five minutes later the back of Palmer's hand was completely free of the burn. Meredith nodded bemusedly in agreement. There could be no of doubt it. No-one could consciously fake that. He listened as Jane Salisbury began to speak calmly and persuasively to the hypnotised man beside her.

'John, I want you to go back through time, a long way back, long before your birth as John Palmer. You are slipping back – ' the man's head moved, he licked his lips '– back through the centuries, to your former life. But as always you'll still be able to hear me and speak to me. You are still linked with me in this room where your present body is resting comfortably. Do you understand?'

In words seemingly borne on a wind over long distances, his lips barely moving, Palmer murmured 'Yes, I understand.'

'Go back until you are Sir William Harrington.'

'I am Sir William Harrington.'

'It is the year of our Lord fourteen hundred and eighty-five. You are at Market Bosworth just before the battle.'

Meredith's head came up with a jerk, his eyes wide. A myriad half-formed questions jostled for utterance. Bourne grinned tightly.

'Yes, Meredith, Bosworth Field. Where King Richard joined battle with Henry, Earl of Richmond. Your history speciality.'

'Who is this William Harrington?'

Bourne slowly shook his head, a finger across his lips, advocating silence.

Jane spoke. 'Go forward in time to the battle, Sir William. It has begun. King Richard holds Richmond at bay. The King depends upon Lord Stanley coming to his aid with his men for he holds Lord Stanley's son George as hostage for his support.'

Meredith thought: Stanley, devious, self-seeking, treacherous Stanley, who played both sides against the middle, who hung back hoping to come in on Richmond's or Richard's side if either showed clear signs of winning. As he did. But who is Sir William? The name was familiar but he could not quite place the knight. Jane was still speaking.

'You've just left the messenger. What did he tell you?'

Palmer's voice was strangely rough. Beads of sweat budded on his forehead. His dark hair seemed damp. With a shock Meredith saw that his face seemed changed. It was harder, stronger, more primitive.

'George has escaped. The messenger – ' His brow furrowed in bewilderment. 'The messenger says George has escaped York, is wounded, in hiding. Tell his father. I must tell Lord Stanley.' He frowned. 'I must go and tell Lord Stanley.'

'Quickly now.' The woman leant over Palmer in emphasis. 'The battle is raging. Take horse. Go and tell Lord Stanley. He must be told now.' She paused. Meredith felt his mouth dry with a terrible foreboding. There was perhaps ten long seconds of silence. During that time interval Meredith seemed to live on two levels. He was vividly aware of the tableau before him in the quiet room, Salisbury in her long blue evening gown, arms bare, leaning over Palmer shrunk into the sofa corner; Bourne, master of ceremonies, seated complacently behind the large desk while Maitland, head bent like an acolyte at prayer, watched the gently-turning spools of the recorder. He also was aware of every agonising phase of the Battle of Bosworth Field, the great, decisive conflict he had studied so thoroughly, that ended the vicious Wars of the Roses. He had visited the battlefield on a cold, rainy August day, had visualised Richmond's forces gathering near Tamworth with Stanley's men arrived at Atherstane. Richard had force-marched from Nottingham to Leicester, reaching it on August 20th. And then the murderous, confused conflict at Bosworth had begun, with Richard and Richmond rallying their exhausted men as they stabbed, hacked, speared, axed each other, slipping on grass wet with blood and entrails, sweating, gasping, cursing, shouting rallying cries, screaming in agony as swords pierced them, in a seemingly endless maelstrom of mindless butchery. While nearby Stanley's restless forces watched and awaited their Lord's decision.

He heard the woman speak once more.

'Sir William, go forward in time one month. It is one month after the battle of Bosworth Field. It is September 20th. Who won?'

Meredith saw Palmer's (Sir William's?) head lean back. Tears streamed down his face. His lips snarled back in agony from irregular teeth.

'King Henry. Sweet Jesu forgive me. I was bewitched. The messenger was false or straight from Hell. What ailed me? I was King Richard's faithful puirsuivant. And was back beside him in the final heat of battle.'

'You *are* there. What is happening.'

The man's voice rose, his face was sweat-sheened, his body jerked uncontrollably, a fly trapped in a web of emotion.

'The Stanleys attack us. Their forces are too strong for us. The King's horse is down.' Palmer's voice was almost a scream. 'Sire, sire! The day's lost. Go now! Another day will come. You must leave! Take my horse, sire, and go! Rebuild your forces and take again what is rightfully yours.' He sobbed uncontrollably, his head lashing from side to side. 'No!' he shouts. 'I'll take your horse, good Sir William, but never flee. My battle-axe is in my hand and the crown of England on my helm, and by Him Who made both land and sea, as King of England I will die!' The man wept. He drew a deep rasping breath. 'They stripped him, flung his body across a pony, like … like … a dead deer.' The voice broke. 'It was not right. It was not … right.'

The silence in the room was broken by the man's harsh sobs.

Meredith sat stunned. At length he found his voice.

'But this is not what happened. The messenger who

convinces Sir William to tell Lord Stanley his son is safe is not a historical figure. This is a complete fabrication – '

'True – in part. The messenger is a fabrication but Sir William believes him to be real. And Sir William therefore acted – much against his wishes, I admit. It took quite some time to convince him, I assure you.'

'But what you are saying? Sir William told a different story originally? And you – ?'

'When we discovered Sir William we got an account of potentially great historical interest. To have an eye-witness to one of the most interesting periods in English history, the end of the bloody and devastating Wars of the Roses, the crucial battle in Bosworth Field, the beginning of that long sunny period of peace and stability in which England flourished as never before.' Meredith thought again, *Now is the winter of discontent / made glorious summer by this sun of York.* Indeed, it had been. Meredith's own great thesis, the one that had finally established his world-wide reputation as the foremost historian of the period, had been an exhaustive and perceptive account of the half-century following Richard III's victory at Bosworth Field. With his massive talents already evident from his successful administration at York, his flair for reconciliation, his courage and capacity for hard work, his thoughtful agnosticism and philosophical bent, Richard during his long reign had done more than any other man to weld the former warring factions into one nation in which the arts and sciences, commerce and the standard of living of the ordinary citizen blossomed as never before. But Bourne was speaking, eyes gleaming with self-satisfaction.

'Oh, we milked Sir William of everything he knew. It took weeks. It's all on tape. It gave us a host of new insights into life in the late fifteenth century, I can tell you. In fact we haven't really digested or assessed it all thoroughly yet. It'll render out-of-date quite a few theses of the period.' His eyes darted a glance at Meredith.

'But according to Sir William, Richard III was killed at

Bosworth.'

'Ah yes. It was Peter who wondered about that. One night
after a session with Sir William, Peter – Well, Peter. Speak for
yourself.'

The man by the recorder switched it off, scratched his
rather prominent nose.

'It arose in a curious way. Arnold was asking Sir William
about a particular historical matter.' He paused, frowned. 'Oh
yes! He asked Sir William if Sir James Tyrrel of Gipping was at
Bosworth. And Sir William said: "No. He arrived the next
morning." And then he added: "I told you that last time we
talked." And Jane said, "Now who is remembering this? The Sir
William entity surfacing in John's body under hypnosis or the
real Sir William in the fifteenth century? It is possible *he* has some
new memories as well?" '

Jane Salisbury nodded. 'Yes. We batted it around for a
time. It really became quite a philosophical monkey puzzle of a
question. Was it possible that in some way we had a bridge to the
fifteenth-century Sir William? If so, could we actually influence
him – the real Sir William – to alter his life, change a decision.
And if so ...' She shrugged, looked at Bourne.

'And if so,' he repeated slowly, 'What would it do to
history?'

Meredith found himself gnawing at a thumbnail.

'But there's another point.'

'Yes?'

'Who does Sir William think he's talking to?'

'Ah, yes. Good question. We asked him. He said, "I do
but dream and in such dreams, shadow people good and evil
converse with me." '

'Then in such circumstances, would the fifteenth-century
Sir William pay attention to voices in his dreams?'

'Probably not. We saw that. So we really worked hypnoti-
cally on him. Yes. We actually hypnotised Sir William. Over a
number of sessions we planted what I've come to think of as the
mirror image of a post-hypnotic suggestion in the John Palmer

Sir William's mind which would surface half-way through the battle in the real Sir William's mind.' Bourne smiled. 'Sir William, totally convinced that he had been told by a messenger that George Stanley had escaped, and totally conditioned into galloping to George's father to tell him his son was no longer being held as hostage by Richard, did so. Afterwards, no longer in thrall to us, in the total confusion, he rejoined the battle to fight at Richard's side. And Lord Stanley, no longer restrained to stand on the sidelines, brought his forces in on Richard's side.'

'But in God's name why? What were you trying to do?'

'To show that if we managed to change the past, nothing much would happen.' Bourne got up. 'We're still here. Everything is as before. It shows that the flow of history cannot be diverted easily. Details change. Oh yes. But the great economic forces and all those other factors talked about at dinner dominate everything.'

Meredith thought feverishly for a moment.

'But would we know?'

'What do you mean?'

'If history was changed would we know? Wouldn't all records be changed, inorganic *and* organic? Papers, books, chronicles, … human memories? Those people we meet in this life are the ones we would meet in the altered world because this would be the altered world. Those events we experience are the right ones for the world we inhabit now. Those buildings we live in or visit are the real ones for that world. Everything is consistent because it has to be. We wouldn't know.'

Bourne gestured with his right hand as if flicking away an annoying mosquito. Obviously he hadn't an answer. Meredith saw a look of doubt appear on Jane Salisbury's face. She frowned.

'You mean – ?'

'Any change, tiny detail or major, could not be detected for we are *all* the products of the world those changes made.' For one blissful moment Meredith thought he'd understood the mechanism, he'd solved the time paradox, the nightmare had been dispelled. And then, like a bomb-defusing soldier who sees the fatal mistake he has made in the microsecond before being blown to oblivion, the realisation hit him, hit him in an assembling of events he had totally forgotten. His stomach churned, a taste of copper tainted his mouth and he knew the blood was draining from his face. They all saw the change in his features. With dry mouth he asked:

'How long ago did you plant in Sir William's mind the post-hypnotic suggestion?'

Jane answered. 'Four days ago. Arnold got in touch with you the following morning.'

'Does your belief that you actually reached Sir William at Bosworth depend only on the episode of taking him a month forward to September 20th?'

'Why yes.'

'No further?'

'No.'

'So you haven't researched his post-Bosworth life in the world where Richard was killed?'

'No. Of course we followed him to the end of his life in this world. He dies in obscurity in 1497 on a visit to France.' She gasped. 'I see! If we're living in Henry of Richmond's world,' she rubbed her forehead slowly, 'either our memories haven't changed as you said they would or Sir William didn't really alter history. It was a fantasy.' The smile of relief froze on her face as she read the numbed expression on Meredith's. Her voice was hushed. 'There's something else, isn't there?'

'Yes. Clifford's theorem.'

'Clifford's theorem?'

'Yes. Nothing can travel faster than the velocity of light.'

'What's that got to do with it?' Bourne's voice was truculent.

'You meddling, stupid, irresponsible, arrogant fool.' Meredith surprised himself at the venom in his voice. 'You've really done it. Of course we'd still remember – for a time. Of course we'd still be living our unaltered lives – for a time. When Sir William set in motion the events culminating in the defeat of

Richard, the changes they began would – will – propagate through space-time at a speed governed by the speed of light at most. You, and your fellow meddlers, set up, yes, a literal time-bomb. I don't really understand it yet, but it'll be like a dam breaking with the flood of changes careering along a myriad different channels at speeds dependent on the terrain. Oh, I don't suppose in the fifteenth and sixteenth centuries' loosely-knit social structure the changes will be universal, even in England. Apart from the sudden disappearance or appearance of a few men, women and children, life will not be too disturbed except at the top of the social scale. It could well be attributed to witchcraft. But as it goes on through time it will grow. My God! How it will grow. Because of the multitude of 'paths' and various consequences caused by previous changes the change will begin to hit us in the present era quite gradually, then grow cataclymis-cally until appearances, disapppearances, destruction of build-ings, creation of new ones, ships, planes, trains, vehicles flicker in and out of existence, often even trying to occupy the same time-space coordinates. It's impossible to imagine. It'll be a never-ending chaotic hell. Oh, the planet will survive but all the work of mankind and the race itself probably won't.'

Bourne licked his lips.

'I can't believe it is as bad as that.'

'Can't you, you fool?' In total conviction Meredith said: 'If you were to take your categories of former life subjects century by century from Bosworth onwards and regress them now, you'd find them singing a different tune.' His grin was a rictus of irony. 'You could actually monitor the progress of the wave-change.' He had that vivid image again of a dam bursting, with observers scattered over the doomed landscape below it, ceasing to communicate by telephone as the floodwaters over-whelmed them one by one with those farther downstream.

'Yes. You could do that – if you had time.'

But Bourne was not yet convinced.

'What do you mean – if we had time?'

'Can't you see. It's already begun to reach us.' Meredith

recalled the graphic tabloid accounts he'd read on the morning train from York. 'The current so-called world-wide terrorist atrocities are only the first tremors of change. It's begun. People are disappearing in increasing numbers or appearing and being treated as madmen for the wild stories they tell. Buildings are being destroyed, communications disrupted, machinery exploding. It's begun to reach us. And it's snowballing. Fast.'

Bourne, Maitland and Jane stared frozen-faced at Meredith. Palmer, or Sir William, was still locked in his own private nightmare.

Jane's eyes opened wide. 'But we can reverse it! Cancel it! We can take John back again to Sir William's time and remove the post-hypnotic suggestion from Sir William.'

'No you can't. You haven't understood yet. You've already started the first wave of change. It's beginning to reach us already. Even if you cancel now, you'll only begin another one to follow the first. It won't even cancel the first one's effects when it reaches any particular era, for those effects are compounded now by its interactions with the status quo. No. You've really gone and done it this time.' He looked at their stunned faces before turning to make for the door. Opening it, he turned again and took a last look at them. His tones were acid with bitterness as he spoke. 'And now, I wish you a good night. For I don't think I want to see any of you again.'

In the early morning sunshine Meredith sat on a bench at the railway station, waiting for his train to York. He had little expectation that it would appear on schedule but it might. He intended in any event to try to get back to York and face in Richard's old city whatever the change-wave would bring. In his hand was his old, well-worn copy of Shakespeare's *Richard III*. He browsed through the familiar pages. Would there be a Shakespeare after the change? Would he be a playwright and even write a version of Richard's short reign and early death? Could be. The change-wave would surely not be totally disruptive by 1593. He remembered suddenly that George Stanley, the ex-hostage, had married the heiress of a Lord Strange and a descendent had been the patron of the company of actors that first produced the play *Richard III*. After the death of Lord Strange in 1594 the company became the Lord Chamberlain's men. All such useless knowledge now. He opened the book at Act V, scene IV at the great soliloquy of Richard, made after the victory at Bosworth Field.

> *Now is the winter of our discontent*
> *Made glorious summer by this sun of York;*
> *And all the clouds that lour'd upon our house*
> *In the deep bosom of the ocean buried.*
> *Too long hath England warred and scarr'd herself;*
> *The brother blindly shed the brother's blood.*
> *The father rashly slaughter'd his own son,*
> *The son, compell'd, been butcher to the sire:*
> *All this divided York and Lancaster,*
> *Made desolate their lives in dire division.*
> *Now let this house, with fair and prosperous days*
> *Enrich the time to come with sooth-fac'd peace.*
> *Let civil wound be stopp'd, peace live again:*
> *That she may long live here, God say amen!*

Meredith closed the book and thought of the King of England mounted on good Sir William's horse, beginning his last charge, battle-axe in hand, the gold circlet of kingship on his helm.

Again in his mind he heard that great shout of resolution in the face of shameful treachery, the full ramifications of which he would never know.

'King of England I will die!'

Meredith promised himself that in the coming days of evil he would strive to keep that picture firmly in the forefront of his mind.

HISTORICAL NOTES

In our time-line, of course, Glasgow University, founded in 1451, 1450 (old style), occupied a site on the High Street only until 1870 when it was transferred to the new buildings on Gilmorehill overlooking the Kelvingrove Park. The Old College entrance Meredith passed through was transferred stone by stone in 1885 to the Gilmorehill site and rebuilt as Pearce Lodge, named after the wealthy ship-building Sir William Pearce, who paid for its removal and re-erection.

It has always seemed a little odd to me that despite his son George being held hostage by Richard, Lord Stanley should finally, having stood on the side-lines so long at Bosworth, have entered the battle on Richmond's side.

Clifford was a real figure. William Kingdon Clifford was a brilliant mathematician and theoretical physicist of the late 19th century. Pre-Einstein, his papers and his famous book *The Common Sense of the Exact Sciences* suggest that he was well on the way to foreshadowing some of Einstein's celebrated discoveries – if he had not died at an early age from the ravages of pulmonary tuberculosis.

Meredith's recollections regarding the relationship of the descendant of George Stanley and the company of players which first performed Shakespeare's *Richard III* in 1593 are still true for our time.

Richard III is possibly one of the most unjustly maligned figures in history. Henry VII's (and Tudor successors') historians wrote much of the historical accounts of the end of the Plantagenet era on which Shakespeare – living in the Tudor era – based his play. There is even considerable doubt as to whether Richard was guilty of the murder of the little Princes in the Tower of London. Even his enemies agree that he was a talented and brave man who met his death at Bosworth Field fighting courageously to the end. It is not without relevance that after the battle the Town Council of York collectively and bravely stuck its neck out by having inscribed in the Town Annals: *This day was our good King Richard piteously slain and murdered; to the great heaviness of this city.*

Two fascinating examinations of Richard's life and deeds are P. Kendall's *Richard the Third* (1955) and Josephine Tey's *The Daughter of Time* (1951). Both, to put it mildly, cast considerable doubt on the Tudor propaganda painting of Richard as a morally and physically crippled schemer, the fifteenth-century version of a Mafia gangster hell-bent on achieving supreme godfather status.

It is in Josephine Tey's fine book that Sir William Harrington is to be found.

Archie Roy